Finding Peace from Shattered Pieces
(Volume 1)

A Trap Girls Bible

L. S. Taylor

Finding Peace from Shattered Pieces
(Volume 1)

A Trap Girls Bible

Published by Chosen Vessels Publishing & Entertainment (USA) Inc.
Jacksonville, Florida 32210 U.S.A.

First Printing
Copyright © 2020 – LaTeshia S. Taylor
All rights reserved

Chosen Vessels Publishing & Entertainment, Inc.

REGISTERED TRADEMARK

ISBN – 978-0-578-61246-1
Printed in the United States of America

Book Cover by: Oliviaprodesign
Editors: Brittany Thomas, D.C. Whitfield, Iris Mendez

PUBLISHER'S NOTE

This book is a work of Fiction. Names, characters, places, and incidents either are the product of the author's imagination or are used fictitiously, and any resemblance to actual persons, living, or dead, business establishments, events, or locales is entirely coincidental.

Without limiting the rights under copyright reserved above, no part of this publication may be reproduced, stored in or introduced into a retrieval system, or transmitted, in any form, or by any means (electronic, mechanical, photocopying, recording, or otherwise) without the prior written permission of both the copyright owner and the above publisher of this book.

The scanning, uploading, and distribution of this book via the Internet or via any other means without the permission of the publisher is illegal and punishable by law. Please purchase only authorized electronic editions, and do not participate in or encourage electronic piracy of copyrighted materials. Your support of the author's rights is appreciated

Acknowledgements

*F*irst and foremost, I want to thank **God.** I am grateful that "my gift for writing has made room for me." (Proverbs 18:16 A man's gift makes room for him and brings him before the great.)

Secondly, I want to take a moment to acknowledge **my three children**. I want each one of you to know that I love you more than life itself. Please understand that the three of you have ALWAYS been the motivation behind my grind. Everything I've done in my life, whether legal or illegal, was all for you, and I wouldn't change a thing, especially if it means sacrificing your happiness.

I want to acknowledge **my dad,** who will always be my hero. Thank you for keeping your word and caring for us the best way you knew how. Thank you for being a solid example of what a real man is supposed to be.

To my mother, I love you. I forgive you. Thank you for giving me life. I thank you for the positive childhood memories that I hold near and dear. I thank you for allowing me to understand that to be human is to be imperfect. I realize that although addiction is a disease, it is NOT a final destination, and I give God all the glory to restore our relationship.

To my Bonus Mother **Cheryl**, thank you. Although we've had our differences, you made sure we didn't want for anything, and I appreciate you for that. I thank God for healing the broken pieces between us. There's genuinely nothing my God cannot do. And lastly, I thank you for loving my dad the way you do. You showed me early on, a glimpse of what it means to give your spouse unconditional love.

To my sister circle, **Tip, Shey, Nicky, Lorraine, and Dee**. I thank y'all for loving me, flaws, and all. Your loyalty and support throughout the years have meant everything to me. I love y'all so much, and I can honestly say that I never would've made it without the four of you by my side.

J.T. & Mike, *I can't thank y'all enough for always having my back, and loving and protecting me, just as brothers are supposed to. Please know, I'll do the same for y'all if the shoe was ever on the other foot. Y'all are the real MVP's. We ride together, we die together!*

To my bonus bestie, the best editor in the world, ***Brittany****. I would not and could not have done this without your encouragement and support. You took my story to a whole other level, and I thank you immensely for pushing me to get this book done. See you at the top boo; we on our way!*

To my publisher, ***Chosen Vessels International Publishing House, Inc.****, thank you. All the calls, back and forth emails, and meetings did not go unnoticed. I'm sure I was a nuisance, but your support and kindness never wavered.*

*To **J.R.**, thank you for your support, prayers, and affirmations over this body of work. You are appreciated.*

And finally, to my coworkers, social media friends and followers, and family members who've supported me on this journey and purchased this book. I am truly overwhelmed and overjoyed by the amount of support I've received from you. I can't wait to give you more from **L.S. Taylor's "Trap Girls Bible Volume II"** *coming soon!*

Préface

"To a child growing up in the hood, safety and security is an illusion. You never knew what drama would go down, from an argument over something petty, a domestic fight between a woman catching her man with another woman or a tragic drive-by. But when you grow up in the "trap," you learn to accept that, that's just the way it is."

Sitting on the porch steps of any neighborhood residence would reveal everyday hook-ups in the hood. Hook-ups that could be safe or hook-ups that wouldn't be safe. But on this particular day, the hook-up was good! My mom got the hook up from a neighborhood booster when she copped a **Cabbage Patch** *doll for me. I sat on the steps of my house with my new doll brushing her hair. I brushed her hair like my Momma brushed mine, swift and continuously. Only, my* **Cabbage Patch** *doll didn't cry and have a fit like I would when my Momma combed my hair. I hated getting my hair combed! My hair was long and thick.*

It spilled over my chocolate shoulders, that blended with a night sky, wafting a delicate aroma of Crown Royal grease. My cabbage patch doll didn't budge or pull away from the strokes of her hair being brushed. I thought to myself, "If only my Momma would brush and comb my hair the way I do my dolls hair, it would be so easy." Those thoughts were short-lived.

Out of nowhere, a tall, slender white man appeared with a giraffe neck, and a jet-black mustache, that semi camouflaged a single-sided smile that he pulled on. He had stiff, slicked-back hair and a stern stare. As he got closer, his facial expression shifted from serious to a look of discomfort, as if he'd put his shoes on the wrong foot or something. My eyes were fixated on him, "White men don't ever come to our house, so who is this man, and why is he here?" I thought to myself. Never mind why he was really on our steps. He wore a wrinkled blue suit and stained white shirt that was half tucked in, and a tie that didn't match. I knew not to talk to him, though, cause' Momma told me not to ever talk to strangers. So, I didn't.

But he was getting closer and closer, and before you knew it, I found myself scared and wondering why is he standing so close to me? Suddenly he leaned forward, putting his arms on the rail, with his lips slightly parted, as though to get to the bottom. In a dull, flat voice, he said, "Hello Tameka, where is your Momma? May I speak with her?" I briefly glanced up at him, laid my Cabbage Patch doll across my lap, and crossed my arms. I'm thinking, "Who is this man? How does he know my name and Momma?" I knew he wasn't a rich man or one of my Momma's friends. I wanted to ask him how he knew my name. But before I could say a word, he stretched his long legs across the third and final step of our porch, and with one swift kick, he smashed the center of the door so hard it swung wide open, leaving the doorknob sealed into the wall. As soon as he came face to face with my Momma, his breathing was rapid, his mouth tightened. From that point on, I vowed to never trust a white man in a wrinkled suit, period.

Trap Bible 1:1 Protection

Commandment: Honor Thy Sister & Brother

Five-O is what my Momma called them. Police surrounded my house by the dozen or so it seemed. "Thud," the sound that's forever engraved in my mind as he and his friends bum-rushed our house. He slammed my Momma to the floor and handcuffed her right in front of my brothers and me. I was only four years old at the time. I kicked and screamed at these white men. "No, stop hurting her!" I wrapped my arms around my Momma's leg as tight as I possibly could, but the officer was stronger than me, and he pried my little fingers off one by one. "Mommy, mommy!" I screamed. My mom was trying to break away.

"Don't do me like this in front of my kids!" The officer turned a deaf ear and began to read Momma her rights. "You have the right to remain silent. Anything you say, can, and will be used against you in a court of law." As he proceeded to read my Momma her rights, the other officer drug her outside and shoved her into the back of the police car as she screamed, "Jarvis, get your sister, I don't want her to see this." My Momma's voice echoed as she yelled from the back of the unmarked police car too little, too late. I not only saw everything, but I heard her last words to Jarvis, too, *"You better remember what I told you!"*

Momma always made sure to instill the proper principles in both my brother and me in case anything ever went wrong. She always told him to protect me and never to let anyone hurt me. He looked as lost and confused as to what he would do next. But after a few seconds, he found his voice, shrugged, and said, "okay." But Momma couldn't hear him now. Her hand pressed against the back window to the slow-moving police car. All we could do was stare at her as they took her away. He tried to fight back the tears, but they slowly began to roll down his face. But then, the window rolled down and one last time, *"Protect your sister!"* She yelled one last time, then the car picked up speed and drove her away.

My brother was only two years older than me. Jarvis was short and cocky with a whole lot of heart. Momma's words must have made a serious impact because he didn't play the radio when it came to me. He made sure he kept his word at being my protector every step of the way, just as our Momma had instructed him. I stood there, frozen in disbelief. I watched as the car vanished. Somehow in my heart, I knew my Momma wasn't coming back home that day. But little did I know this would be the first of many trips to the prison my Momma would take.

I knew that very day, my life as I knew it would never be the same. In my childlike thoughts, somehow I realized that the Momma I knew and loved, would become a woman I barely knew and would hardly recognize.

My Momma's sins became the debts of her sons and me, and it wouldn't be long until we figured that out for ourselves.

Trap Bible 2:2 Accusation

Commandment: Thou Shall Not Steal (My Momma) From Me

Cool as a cucumber, Attorney Constance stood for her opening statement and walked up to the Judge, where the curious crowd behind her could listen in. "My client has previously been guilty of forgery." She paused to look at the jurors then continued even louder. "Although she is innocent." The crowd behind her gasped. "Until proven guilty," Constance continued, with one finger high in the air," Ms. Buchanan should know better." With full force, she slammed her hand on the opposing attorney's desk.

Attorney Constance called witnesses to the stand concerning the facts in the case. After questioning the witnesses, the defendant then cross-examined the witnesses.

"Please state your name for the record."

"Jessica Blackshear. "

"Can you please confirm that you're the respondent in the civil case file #74587?"

"I am."

"You're working as a retail cashier for Dillard's Department store, in the Regency Square Mall. Is that correct?"

"Yes, ma'am."

"Is the defendant in this courtroom someone you can recall purchasing items at your check out register on Saturday, June 27?" She looks in Momma's direction and nods her head. She was shaking like a stripper.

"Would you please answer the question with a yes or no?"

"Yes. I recognize the defendant as a customer that day."

"Do you recall how the items purchased were paid? With Cash, Credit Card, Debit Card, or a Check?"

"A check was used. It had to be input by hand because it would not clear through the automated system."

"What type of identification is needed to purchase items with a check?"

"A driver's license."

"What type of identification was used by the defendant?"

"A driver's license was used for identification."

"When you checked the picture on the driver's license, do you recall the person purchasing the items and the picture on the license being the same person?"

"To my knowledge . . . It all was happening so fast. It looked like her."

"Do you know anyone else who can shed light on this incident?"

Nervously…Ms. Blackshear answered.

"No." She hesitated. "Not that I can think of." Jessica Blackshear shook her head.

"Is there anything else you want to tell me that I haven't asked you?"

"I, I, don't know." Jessica fidgeted.

"Did you attend high school with the defendant during your sophomore year?

"I didn't know her that well back then."

"So does that statement mean that you know her better presently?"

Attorney Constance jumped to her feet, "Objection, Your Honor. Counsel is misleading the witness." The attorney smirked at Attorney Constance. "Overruled." Said the Judge.

The attorney said, "I have no further questions for the witness."

Once the evidence was received, both attorneys summarized the case in their closing statements. After the closing statements, the Judge explained to the jury that they must "make their decision based on the facts presented and not their feelings." They must all agree on a verdict of GUILTY or NOT GUILTY.

The jury came back out in only ten short minutes. The Judge said, "Will the Defendant and defense Counsel stand. "Members of the jury, have you reached a verdict?" The jury spokesman stood and said, "Yes, your Honor, we have.

The Judge then asked, "Members of the Jury, in the case of the State of Florida vs. Lucille Tiggs, what do you say?"

The Jury Spokesman cleared his throat before pronouncing, "Your Honor, the members of this Jury find the defendant GUILTY of forgery."

Loud conversations burst out within the room. Most came from my Momma's family and friends. The Judge had to bang her gavel several times before there was peace again. "Order! Order in my courtroom!" She said in a stern voice.

Although I wasn't old enough to know what this meant for my family and me, I could tell something wasn't right by the look on my Momma's face. I wondered, *"Who are all these people crowded around my Momma? Why are they asking her all these questions? And why can't I be with her?"* I thought to myself, if my brothers and I thought our lives had changed on that day as we watched them throw our Momma in the back of that unmarked police car, we would have never imagined the pain that was soon to come.

Micah, the youngest, was only two years old at the time of our Momma's trial. He didn't have a clue about what was going on. For a moment, I wished I was in his shoes. I didn't know everything about Momma, but the fact that I knew something made me feel uneasy. As I began to reflect on the situation, I realized, *"How are we supposed to tell Micah about Momma if we don't even know what happened ourselves?"* My four-year-old thoughts were all over the place. *"Snap out of it!"* I thought.

"It is time." The Judge said this statement with finality.

"I agree with the jury on the verdict of guilt, and now sentence Lucille Tiggs to five years in the Florida State Correctional Facility for Women!" My family and I watched closely as the sheriff put handcuffs on my Momma and took her away. This was the start of it all.

I never really knew what my Momma did to be away from us, and the word forgery was as foreign to my ears as Spanish. But as I grew older, I would often hear folks talk. The report on the streets was, she forged signatures and cashed stolen checks. This information hit me deep. I couldn't picture the woman that I loved doing something that extreme. It seemed as if the world was playing a sick joke on me. Were the accusations true, or was this a case of mistaken identity?

Now I was faced with the reality that both of my parents were behind bars. I couldn't imagine or think what the future held for my brothers and me. Would we ever be a family again? Would we be forced to split up? Those were questions I pondered in the back of my mind.

My dad was already making an eight-year bid for aggravated battery. He damn near beat a man to death. I was only an infant when he left, so he wasn't to my knowledge, at least, a pivotal figure in my life. But Momma was different because Momma was always there. When I was happy, she was there. When I was sad, she was there. Anytime I needed her, she was there. And now, nothing! This situation was way too much for a child my age. So, I can only imagine how Jarvis felt.

My Grandmomma, my daddy's Momma, became our caretaker. To help ease some of the pain and sudden changes in our lives, she took us to see our daddy every Sunday. He always promised to take care of my brothers and me when he came home from prison. And although our hearing his promises made us happy, his freedom wasn't sure for at least another five years.

As time passed, I slowly witnessed the divide between my brothers and me. My baby brother Micah did not have the same daddy as Jarvis and I. That biological difference sent Micah to live with his uncle on his dad's side, who later adopted him. Ten long years would pass before we would ever see each other again.

Trap Bible 3:3 Provision

Commandment: Thou Shall Not Bite the Hand that Feeds You

It never ceased to amaze me how our Grandmomma managed to take care of my brother and me as well as providing for her children. See, my Grandmomma had eleven children. There were six girls and five boys. My dad was the oldest of the boys, and as he grew older, he developed a ruthless reputation in the streets. Living a life of crime for him was like getting high on drugs. He was known for robbing and shooting anyone that stood in his way. It provided instant gratification. Gratification he felt he needed, being the oldest of the male children, which meant he held most of the responsibility and pressure to provide for his family, in his hands. Especially since there was no father figure in the picture.

It's not natural for a child to feel like a burden without cause. But this is what I felt. I couldn't stop wanting things to return the way they were. Jarvis and I wanted and needed our Momma and daddy. But at this point, all we had was each other.

I was worried that my Grandmomma would hold his criminal ways against us. That never happened; she took care of us as a Grandmomma would. My Grandmomma respected how our daddy cared for his siblings, and that showed in the way she raised us. He took care of his family before and during his incarceration, so in turn, she took care of us.

Even as a kid' I couldn't help but feel that Jarvis and I were in the way. Not that my Grandmomma indicated it. I just felt lost without my Momma. If guilt could be what I felt at such a young age, then guilt it was. My Grandmomma had two extra mouths to feed. I didn't feel right.

Trap Bible 4:4 Second Chance

Commandment: Thou Shall Not Take God's Grace for Granted

Over the next five years, we would develop a brother-sister bond like no other. Our connection was strong and unbreakable. It was hard to understand why God allowed my brother and me to witness inappropriate behaviors of adults that we saw. However, who would've known that the deeply-rooted brother-sister bond we shared and developed would keep us from being in the same situations as our parents. My brother had my back, and I had him, right or wrong, we were together.

Days eventually turned into weeks, and weeks into months. Before I knew it, the months morphed into years, and we still never got to visit our Momma. Not a day went by that I did not wonder why we could see our daddy every single Sunday, but we couldn't see our Momma?

Flashbacks invaded my mind often. Especially the day Momma went to court. The scene of Momma dragged out of the courtroom repeated itself in my head over and over again.

There was a reoccurring pain in my chest that had become all too familiar. Whenever I thought about Momma going to jail, I remember my legs being too short for my feet to touch the floor. I recalled only a few people in the rows behind our family. But they weren't people I knew or recognized. With my full attention directed at Momma, I questioningly observed one of the officer's clamp something shiny and silver to both of her legs one at a time and then her hand.

Her attorney hoped that the judge would consider Momma having three small children. The attorney hoped it would possibly change the judge's mind. We were surprised because it seemed to have worked. She only received the minimum five-year prison term. Even though it was a relief for us, the judge made sure to give Momma a lecture before she left the courtroom. "You know, I can do much worse to you, Ms. Tiggs. So I expect much more from you after your release is final." The judge went on to ask, "Does it even bother you, knowing that three beautiful faces are looking up at you, right here in the front row?" Momma looked at us from the corner of her eyes with her head lowered in shame. "What type of example are you setting for them? As a Momma of three young boys myself, I could not imagine putting my children through the pain and agony your children will experience at your cost!" Momma kept her head down and never looked up at the judge.

"Ms. Tiggs, I don't want to hurt you, I simply want you to learn self-respect. If you can't do this for yourself, improve for the sake of your children." Her last effort to get what she was saying through to my Momma was, "Bottom line Ms. Tiggs, people NEVER get a second chance in my courtroom. So consider yourself lucky.

Following the loud slam of her gavel, most began to exit the courtroom. My family slowly gathered together to leave, as well. Still, my full attention was on Momma, and I questioningly observed one of the officer's clamp something shiny and silver to both of her legs one at a time. CLINK! With her hands restrained next as they approached the exit door, all the feelings that I had not felt before surfaced. I covered my face, not wanting to see, and within an instant, I heard CLINK! And peeked through my fingers out of curiosity, just as Momma's face cringed.

I didn't understand why my brother and I were allowed to witness our Momma's downfall. I wanted to get her attention, but they wouldn't let her look in our direction, we didn't even get a chance to say goodbye. They whisked Momma away and swiftly escorted us out of the courtroom to prepare for the next case.

Trap Bible 5:5 Motherless

Commandment: Thou Shall Not Betray the Family

My Grandmomma sensed I was sad. Once we arrived at her house, she explained the best she could to understand what my brother and I had witnessed in court.

"Baby, I know Ya'll children are too young to understand, but your Momma's attorney, the lady in the dark grey pant suit," I nodded my head. "Well, she thought to have her children present during the trial would soften the judge and lessen your Momma's sentence." I looked up at her, puzzled. My young mind was filled with a plethora of questions that I couldn't ask because I didn't know how to. Her sentence wasn't a *slap on the wrists* and ninety days like a petty criminal received. She faced a maximum fifteen-year sentence.

Although I was only a child, I quickly noticed the sudden attitude adjustment my Grandmomma took when discussing anything that had to do with our Momma. She seemed bitter just at the mention of my Momma's name. I wouldn't dare question her about it because in black families, it's an unspoken rule, not to question our elders. It was not until years later that I found out the root of my Grandmomma's hostility toward her.

Before my Momma's first arrest, she lived a life full of crime and heavy drug use. If you've ever been affiliated with the *game* in any way, you'd know what I mean when I say: *"By any means necessary."* Similar to my father, *my mom lived life, not caring about consequences during that time.* I can honestly say crime had her wrapped around its finger. She was too far gone to escape. The *game* was the only life she knew. My dad was away serving time to complicate the situation further, and my Momma found comfort in the arms of another man. This man would eventually become my baby brother Micah's biological daddy. But what infuriated my Grandmomma was not that

Micah had a different daddy from Jarvis and me, everyone knew that. Plus, everyone knows that it's hard to stay ten toes down when facing as much time as daddy was facing. Eventually, you're gonna' crave companionship. So, it's not uncommon to have a "*Boyfriend #2*" or a "*Side Nigga*" as they say in the hood. But instead, what infuriated her, was who Momma's new boo was. Her new boo's name was Melvin. He was a tall, slender, mild-mannered man who seemed perfect for her to the unknown. However, the twist in this situation was that Micah's daddy and my daddy were first cousins!

My Momma and Micah's daddy's relationship represented the ultimate sign of betrayal to my Grandmomma. My family members believed at a very early age that family should stick together. Crossing each other's boundaries was something you knew not to do! It was a sign of respect.

However, when my Momma and Melvin decided to become intimate, they entered into a web of deceit that would backfire in more ways than one. Our family no longer trusted either of them once they found out. Their deception also led to the demoralization and dismemberment of our close-knit family.

Once the truth was exposed, I encountered my first out-of-body experience. At that moment, I believe I understood my Grandmomma's rage. So much so, I found myself uneasy. Imagine the confusion you experience when you discover that your baby brother is also your little cousin. What the fuck! What a strange turn of events, right?

I knew the consequences would not be good for either of them once our entire family found out. But I didn't make that bed, so it wasn't mine to lie in. However, it still cut deep because regardless of the situation, that was My Momma.

My genuine concern for my Momma's well-being quickly outweighed the fears of what my family was capable of. Before I knew it, two years had passed and still…no visit to mama. I can't speak for everyone else, but I know for me, this was pure torture. As with any challenging experience in life, some days were much harder than others. There were days I felt a sense of confidence like I can do anything I put my mind to. I thought my brothers where the only people I needed besides myself. I guess you can say I felt a sense of contentment. However, more often than none, I experienced days longing for a Momma I barely remembered, and the sadness accompanied by a few memories I did possess. During this time, it seemed as if no one could understand what I was going through. Not being able to receive my Momma's guidance or hear her voice every day began to take a toll on me. All of the people around me had both of their parents, or so it seemed. And amid everyone else was me.

A broken, confused, and seemingly parentless little girl tried to piece together things I wasn't even old enough to comprehend. I thought back to life before my mama left. Every day she would sit me in front of the mirror and brush my hair. After each soft stroke of the brush, she would whisper in my ear, "You're so beautiful." I slid my fingers through my hair as I reminisced. Or she would say to me, Baby, it's okay, get back up and try again." Every time I fell off my bike. Having her to comfort me always made the pain go away. However, these days, the pain seems to linger.

And to make matters worse, that lingering pain was slowly turning into resentment. I saw this coming forth; however, I no longer cared enough even to try and heal it. Maybe it's because no one ever seemed to care how I felt anyway, or so I thought. And if they did care, they didn't put a lot of effort into proving it. I always assumed that because I was young at the time of my parent's arrest, everyone thought I was indifferent towards the situation, but I wasn't.

However, in the years to come, EVERY PERSON in my path was about to find out how angry I was. The first day of school was steadily approaching. I was excited about what was to come but also a bit nervous about my transition to the "Big School," as my brother Jarvis would call it. I remembered last year; he would come from school every day, telling me how much fun he would have. Out of all the kids that stayed with Grandmomma, I was the youngest. So most days, it was just her and I in the house by ourselves. I didn't mind, though, because Grandmomma was a lot of fun. Every day, at noon sharp, my Grandmomma and I would tune into her favorite game show *Family Feud*. *Family Feud* was my Grandmomma's favorite show. I loved to watch how engaged she was, from the time the opening of the credits rolled until the host said his farewells.

I couldn't wait for someone to give a ridiculous answer so that I could sneak a laugh in as my Grandmomma griped and cursed at the television screen. "We asked a survey of one hundred people, name something better than being rich?" Asked the host. "Now Darla, keep in mind, you guys have two strikes. One more strike and the other team could steal and win the game." He said, in suspense. Nervously Darla replied, "Umm, being poor!" The buzzer sounded. Darla had babbled; she didn't even realize what she said until it was too late. On cue, my Grandmomma sounded off. "Being poor… lady, what kind of BULLSHIT is that? I've been poor all my goddamn life, and it ain't nothing fun about it." She stared blankly at the television screen.

"Shit, give me the twenty thousand dollars so that I can slap her clear across her face, with each hundred-dollar bill one by one!" We both glanced at each other and laughed, for this was our bonding time. The little time I had with my Grandmomma during, the day was a part of the reason that I preferred watching what I considered "old people shows" over watching cartoons. These were the times I felt wanted the most.

Trap Bible 6:6 Encouragement

Commandment: Thou Shall Take Love as It Comes

Finally, the first day of school had arrived. Jarvis walked me to my classroom. My classroom was a portable behind the school. I didn't want him to leave me, so I started to cry. In tears, I heard a soft voice not far behind my brother and me. The woman said, "It's okay sweetie, I can handle it from here, go to your class young man." Jarvis hesitated but slowly walked down the ramp of the portable.

I stood there shaken. When I looked up, I saw this tall, slender lady in a blue and white polka dot dress standing in front of me. She reached for my hand while standing in the slightly opened classroom door. Usually, very shy and timid, I was surprised at myself as I took her hand as she led me into the classroom.

There was something about her personality that gave me a sense of security. I felt warmth as she walked me to my seat. I sighed, relieved as I sat in my desk, which was placed close to Mrs. Morton's desk, or at least that's how it felt.

So far, kindergarten was going okay. The school became an outlet for me. It was the place where I received the most attention. Although the majority of it was for misbehaving or disrupting the class, it still strangely fulfilled my needs. I wasn't concerned with whether I was good or bad. I just wanted someone to pay attention to me. I looked forward to getting in trouble. Because I knew someone would be concerned with my feelings and why I was the way I was.

Receiving attention was what comforted me on most days. So, I was willing to do whatever it took to get the attention I felt I deserved. However, no matter how much I acted out, Mrs. Morton was always so patient with me. Her patience was foreign to me, and I liked it. "Tameka, sweetie, what's wrong? Are you having a bad day? She got up from her desk and walked over to where I was seated. "Do you want to sit a little closer to Mrs. Morton today and be a big girl?" She asked. I would light up like a bulb and smile. I said, "Yes, ma'am." She arranged my desk to be even closer to her desk. I could sense the other student's envy. But I didn't care. I wanted and needed my teachers' undivided attention. "Okay, Tameka, I will let you be my little helper, but you have to promise me that you are going to be good for the rest of the day?" I nodded my head in agreement. She was never harsh with me, and that's what I loved the most about her. Her voice was always soft and concerning when she approached me, I needed that. Mrs. Morton would always pull me aside and tell me how smart and beautiful I was, just like Momma used to do. Mrs. Morton's care and concern made me feel good; the same way my Momma would make me feel.

Being around, Mrs. Morton, every day, made me long for my Momma even more. I missed my Momma so much! I was only six-years-old. I didn't know how to express myself. I felt hurt and abandoned, alone, and unwanted. Nothing could replace the emptiness I felt inside. I missed doing girly things with my Momma, being around her every day, and having her home. However, what I missed most was the feeling that someone loved me. I think that's why I loved Mrs. Morton so much, simply because she reminded me so much of Momma. Mrs. Morton always made sure to encourage me. She even gave me treats on my good days, which made me feel special even more. I had never been rewarded for a good deed up until then, only chastised for my actions, good or bad. But Mrs. Morton gave me a glimpse of a positive side of life.

Trap Bible 7:7 Affliction

Commandment: Thou Shall NOT Unleash My Wrath

Sunday's for me were like a breath of fresh air. Grandmomma never missed a beat in taking us to visit daddy in prison. Although daddy was away, the family still had high respect for him. My Grandmomma, as well as my dad's siblings, still depended on daddy. He was the peacemaker, the disciplinarian, the daddy-figure, the guardian, and the most pressured.

My Grandmomma instilled fear and respect for my daddy. He kept us all in line.

I can't count when I heard, "Ya'll wait until Jerome comes home, he's gonna get in Ya'lls behinds!"

Time flew, I was in third grade. Grandmomma was beyond fed up with me. At this point, she'd had enough of the constant phone calls and parent-teacher conferences at my expense. But, my Grandmomma was a true "G." She bitched about my behavior, but she didn't snitch to my daddy.

I believe she had hopes that I'd get better, but unfortunately, my behavior only worsened with time. Now faced with the dilemma of what she should do, my Grandmomma decided to reach out to my school for help. The school put me through a short counseling session and made me take all these strange tests.

Finally, after a few weeks, they determined that I had what most call A.D.D. or Attention Deficit Disorder. After they went over the symptoms and causes with Grandmomma, the testers suggested that I needed medication. Before my Grandmomma made any decision regarding whether she wanted to go through with this, she made sure to talk it over with daddy. And man, was my dad pissed off! When I was growing up, research for A.D.D. and other similar disorders was not as advanced as it is today. Back then, being diagnosed with A.D.D., you would be considered a

Special Needs Student. And if medications were needed, you would be regarded as slow, unmotivated, or having a behavior disorder.

Daddy wasn't buying it. "They think we're all crazy." He told my Grandmomma. "There's no way in hell I'm going to allow some strange white man to tell me anything about my daughter! DON'T let them give her NOTHING…I MEAN IT, Momma!" He shouted. I'd never seen or heard my daddy so angry.

My daddy had one year left in prison. While he was still in prison, he threatened to beat my behind if I continued to act up. What I needed was his unconditional love. Instead, he added more fuel to my fire. His words stuck in my brain like a knife. "He's gonna beat me, huh? Well, I'm gonna give him something worth beating me for!" I was angry. And over the next year, my behavior continued to spiral downward.

My big brother Jarvis was the total opposite. He received Honor Certificates and Star Student awards. I brought home a pile of scholarship warnings and teacher referrals. Now, a little older, I made sure that anyone who disregarded my feelings as a toddler experienced my wrath first hand as a young adult. I wanted everyone around me to suffer like I was suffering. I ruined so many relationships I could honestly have cared less. If you were to look me up in the dictionary, my face would be next to the definition of "Reckless." To be reckless means, "To be without thought of danger: marked by a lack of thought about danger or other possible undesirable consequences." I was indeed thoughtless and reckless was indeed me.

Trap Bible 8:8 Free at Last

Commandment: Thou Shall Be Set Free

At last, it was here. The day I'd been waiting for my whole life is essential. I could barely contain my excitement. My daddy's release date had finally come! He had served eight long years in Prison.

My Grandmomma swore that he was a changed man.

I was only an arm baby when he left, so I only went by word of mouth. Now that he was free, and we were face to face, I noticed he was nothing like the ruthless, gun-toting thug everyone said he was.

Instead, he was very respectable and humble. Prison transformed him.

My experience of visiting daddy was seeing him behind a glass partition. I never realized that he was a huge man. My daddy must have worked out every day in jail because he was huge. I know he had to be lifting weights. The picture I saw before he went to Prison was that of a smaller man. The muscles in his arm were the size of cantaloupes. And although he was only twenty-eight at the time of his release, his face appeared weathered and aged beyond his years. I attributed this to the stress of Prison. He would tell us every Sunday, "Prison isn't the place you want to be. If ya' don't listen to anything else, I say, please listen to this, don't ever break my heart and end up in here the way I did." He told us, "Always stick together, and be somebody in life." I was so excited that daddy was home. I was so young when he left. Having him home made me feel safe. What I loved most about my dad was that he always made me feel like his little princess. No matter what his circumstances. Just like Momma, I couldn't imagine daddy doing the things they said he did either. He was my gentle giant. I breathed a sigh of relief.

Like a puzzle, the missing pieces in my life began to fit in the right spot. I wasn't one hundred percent sure of our future, but what I did know was that I didn't have to worry about his absence any longer. My dad's return offered me a sense of peace.

Sadly, my peace only lasted a moment. Whether my dad knew it or not, the innocent baby he left eight years ago had now blossomed into a rebellious preteen who was no longer afraid of anyone, not even my father. To me, the almighty family fearing "Big J" was just an obstacle in my way.

One thing life had taught me over the last few years was how not to care. I was very withdrawn and guarded anyway, so it was easy for me to distance myself from my emotions. Plus, feelings were not something my family discussed. Emotions as we knew it was a sign of weakness, and that was not something I possessed. If that wasn't enough, watching your support system being hauled to Prison, over and over again, can easily contribute to a lack of emotion.

Each time my Momma left, she took another piece of my heart with her. And now, I was a heartless wreck.

During my internal chaos, things were slowly becoming more stable. I say slowly because, for a while, daddy was unable to get a job. His criminal record made it hard for him to get a job. On the bright side, his search would not take long. Daddy went into a partnership with my Uncle Ben who had recently started a Lawn Care business. My daddy transitioned from the thug he once was to a hard-working single father providing for his family.

I commend him because he kept his word to Jarvis and me, taking us in as soon as he got back on his feet. It is now, Mid- August, and my 10th birthday was quickly approaching. I wasn't quite sure of what I wanted for my big day, but daddy was insisting on me having a party. I had never had a party before this because money was always tight for Grandmomma. However, she would always bake me a cake and sing Happy Birthday to me just to let me know it was my special day. I appreciated that because I know she was doing all that she could.

I was excited about my first birthday party, or at least I was until I overheard a conversation between my Grandmomma and my aunt while they were prepping for the party. Word on the streets was, Mama had been home for a few months now, and she was back to her old tricks.

To distract me from that bad news, daddy decided a birthday party was what I needed. Still, I could not believe that Mama was free, and she didn't even come for us. How could she? I thought. Did she not miss us? Was she mad at us for not visiting her? So many questions went through my mind. And these questions, would once again, go unanswered for another 20 years.

To make matters worse, not only was Mama still cashing stolen checks and forging signatures, now she was a crack addict! I couldn't believe what I heard about my Momma. It had gotten to the point where I didn't know what bad news about her would be next.

What other issues could my Momma possibly have? Why is she doing this to herself? Crack, crack echoed in my mind. Why was crack-cocaine her choice of drugs, or why was she using drugs period? What was she hiding?

Was this the reason she hadn't been to see us? Did she think crack was more important than my brother and me?

The truth slowly revealed itself. The woman I cared about was only a façade. She didn't care about us. All she cared about was herself and her stupid addictions. If she cared about us, she would have come to see us. I told myself to mask the pain. But the truth be told, this time I just couldn't. The hurt and abandonment I felt was beyond anything I had ever experienced. Why doesn't she want me? What did I do? I constantly wondered. But only Mama had the answers. My brothers and I were left wishing and hoping for love from a crack-addicted criminal of a Momma.

Trap Bible 9:9 Blurred Lines

Commandment: Thou Shall Not Replace Momma

September 9th, my birthday was finally here. Daddy had managed to place a smile on my face when he surprised me with the **Smurfett** roller skates I wanted. That would not be the only surprise, though; the biggest surprise was yet to come. Since it was daddy's idea to have the party, he made sure everything was perfect for me. By now, all of my aunts had moved out and started their own families, well, all except for my Aunt Trina, who was only a few years older than me. But daddy made sure to invite everyone. He promised that we would be moving soon too, but we were comfortable just having him home.

Everyone had arrived, and the party was moving about as planned. Everyone seemed to be having a good time. As I went outside on the lawn to enjoy my new roller skates, I started to feel happy daddy suggested the party after all. I wanted to tell him how glad I was, but as soon as I approached him, I noticed he was engaged in what looked like a deep conversation with a strange lady he'd invited to my party. She had brought a little girl name Keisha along, giving me someone my age to play with during the festivities. When we went outside to play, Keisha had mentioned to me that the mysterious lady was her big sister.

Miss Charlene was her name. Come to think of it; I had seen her once before at my Uncle Ben's house. She and Uncle Ben's wife were once roommates.

"Daddy! Daddy!" I yelled! As I skated toward him. "Come watch me skate." Having taken his attention away from the conversation, he said, "Okay, baby, let me see what you got!" Just as I turned to skate away, Miss Charlene said, "We're going to work on your manners, young lady, you need to say excuse me when you see grownups talking." I could not believe she was so blunt and she had just met me.. He was my daddy, and if I wanted to ask him to watch me skate. I had every right to do so. Who is she to tell me what to do anyway? She ain't my Momma, I thought to myself. However, not knowing how to respond, I said, "Okay." and skated away. Why are manners so important to her, anyway? My daddy doesn't have a problem with my ways, so why should she?

I could not wrap my head around the fact that she made such a big deal about ten-year-olds manners or lack thereof, but soon, I would find out that was buttering herself up for a role that she was not qualified for, in my book.

As the sun began to set, and all the guest said their goodbyes, I noticed Miss Charlene seemed to have made her way over to the sofa where Grandmomma was sitting. From the looks of it, they were talking about something pretty serious, and a few minutes later, daddy joined in. I was worried. At this time, I was sitting at the dining room table, eating some of the barbecue baby back ribs, baked beans, and potato salad, leftover from my party. I tried to act casual, slowly eating my ribs, as I attempted to listen in on the conversation, without being noticed by Grandmomma. No matter what tricks I tried, she always knew. Before I could even get deep enough in on the conversation, she yelled the usual. "Get out of grown folk's conversation. Ain't nobody talking to you, little girl! Stay in a damn child's place!" Although I was unable to make out what was said, I could tell everything was okay because Grandmomma gave Miss Charlene a big hug and told her, "Thank you." Miss Charlene said, "Good night." Dad walked her out the door and to her car.

My Grandmomma was a very outspoken, boisterous; tell it like it is, kind of woman. Just as my curiosity began to grow, Grandmomma blurted out, "I'm glad he found somebody to help raise yawl cause' lord knows that Mama of yours ain't worth the skin she wrapped in." My heart sank. Grandmomma and her daughters would always bash Mama in front of Jarvis and me. In the beginning. I wanted so bad to defend her and tell them to stop. Did they think we couldn't hear them or something? Who said those kinds of hurtful things in front of a child and then turned around and told them to stay in a child's place.

What was I supposed to do? So many questions haunted me, but as time went on, I realized Momma wasn't coming back, I slowly began to agree. Momma not coming home hurt me, indeed, and it would take my entire life for me to learn, it's not my fault. It was my Momma's; she was the one who ran away from us. Not me. I loved her so much, but she had other things in mind, more important to her than my brothers and I. These addictions consumed her mind. I tried to process what my Grandmomma said. I thought to myself, "Could this be the big move daddy had been promising? Who was this woman that had somehow infiltrated her way into my daddy's life and had become our play, play Step Momma? Who granted her the right? As I started to reflect, I thought back to the comment Miss Charlene made earlier about my manners, and it all made sense. That was her trap. Immediately, I became uncomfortable and uneasy about the move if that was what daddy had planned for us. This is why she was so worried about my manners. She intended to replace our Momma.

Trap Bible 10:10 Broken Fam... ily

Commandment: Thou Shall Love Us as Your Own

She was in her late twenties, and she was only to be addressed as Miss Charlene, or at least when it came to me. I don't know what it was about her. Maybe it was the way she was put together. Perhaps it was her bowed legs and the way she walked that drove men crazy – in any case, there was something very appealing about her, especially to my dad. She wore her hair layered like the singer Anita Baker. Miss Charlene wore all the latest fashions, so she was always fly. She wasn't knock out gorgeous; there was a smoky kind of sensuousness about her. Attractive in a flawed, accessible way. She doesn't stop the party when she walks in, but you'd know she was there.

Miss Charlene was strong, confident, self-sufficient, passionate in her likes and dislikes, loves and hates. When she spoke, you could hear the *Geechee* accent, which was between creole southern and a Caribbean twang. It was difficult for her to pronounce certain words that were either too big for her vocabulary or the dialect. The letter "t" was pronounced as "c." She would say, "He down the *screet.*" instead of down the *street.* But she was quick-witted, so she always knew how to "play it off" with my brothers and me, at least until we got older. But despite her hiccups, it was something about her that kept daddy coming back. I think it had a lot to do with the fact that she didn't have any unnecessary baggage, that came with her, unlike mama.

Besides her Geechee dialect, she didn't have any addictions. She didn't have drama. Hell, she didn't even have children. Whether it was because she couldn't or didn't want children, Miss Charlene didn't have any. She had a younger sister. Keisha. She brought Keisha to my party. We were around the same age. I was surprised my dad invited them to my party. I had no idea he was dating anyone. It never occurred to me he had anyone else in his life other than Jarvis and me. I wondered how long he had known Miss

Charlene? Maybe he wasn't sure he wanted us to meet her, or maybe he felt like most adults, who he shared his extra time with, was his business. That appeared to be the adult way in our family. If you were an adult, a child had nothing to do with your business. We were supposed to stay in our place. Somehow, I felt it was my place and my business. He was our father.

What bothered me the most was how we had gone from living with our Grandmomma, where we felt unwanted to living with Miss Charlene, where we felt even more out of place and unwanted. Did he even know if she had his children's best interest at heart, or was he just whipped? What if she abused us? What would be his reaction? Would he believe her or us?

To make matters worse, this was her house, and homegirl made sure she let us know it. Everything was **"My!"** You never knew what you could or could not use or do in her house. I was miserable. As children Jarvis and I wanted to run around and play, laugh, scream, and enjoy our surroundings like a home should be. But her house wasn't childproof! I didn't want to touch anything in her place, so I stayed in my room most of the time. As long as I was out of her way, she was cool with me. But on the real, it was no way I wanted to live.

It seemed to me she pretended to be a so-called step momma on the surface. But behind closed doors, she lacked the loving, kindness, and nurturing that a mother should have. I took care of myself. She would try to play that motherly role in front of our daddy. But if her ass didn't like kids, why was she fronting? She was barren. She knew nothing about having a child or nurturing. She didn't have a caring bone in her body for children. I started to resent her.

But as time passed and Jarvis and I realized it could be worse, things started getting better. When you've been without the two most important people in your life, having just a glimpse of normalcy gave me hope. We had two parents now. We had a home, our separate rooms. I was no longer different from kids that had a stable lifestyle. Still, I was conflicted. I always hated when my friends would ask me about my biological momma. It's hard loving parents and being ashamed of them at the same time. I wanted to defend my momma in my heart, but on the surface, I hated who she was, in reality, a drug addict. It was embarrassing and hurtful. I made up endless stories about her whereabouts. Sometimes I would tell them she left us with our father and moved away. Id' tell them Miss Charlene was my Momma to cut out all the questioning. To me, Miss Charlene became an escape from reality. Because from the outside looking in, it looked like I had a family, a mom, and a dad. It felt good. It felt familiar, and that was something I hadn't felt in a long time.

Trap Bible 11:11 Pretend Momma

Commandment: Thou Shall Not Pretend to Love Me

Have you ever felt satisfied when things you've hoped for fall in place? In the hood, we call this "A come up."

Well, this began to happen for my brother and me. We sat back and watched as our lives changed for the better, or so we thought. We graduated from being piled up in one bunk bed or worst-case scenario, sleeping on the floor. We now had separate rooms. Our rooms were decorated entirely, with all the things we loved. My room was painted a pastel pink with white accents. I had a toy chest, both daddy and Miss Charlene had purchased, filled with every type of doll my heart desired. A girl could get used to this. My brother, Jarvis's room, was painted a royal blue with sports decorations along the walls. He, just like me, also had toys he liked. He had all types of cool trucks and cars; he had a basketball hoop hooked to his closet. When he would leave, I would sneak and play with his toys for fun. For the first time in our young lives, it felt as if we were in Heaven. If that wasn't enough, each of our rooms had a TV and boom box. That excited us even more. At Grandmomma's, all of us had to share one TV. Shoot, to top it off, and we went from standing in lines for donated toys at charity centers on Christmas Day to us having our own "real" Christmas at home. Complete with a big green pine tree as tall as the ceiling and presents that spilled from under the tree onto the living room floor. When we walked into the house, you could smell the fresh pine from the leaves. Because of Miss Charlene's flashy nature, Jarvis and I had every material thing we wanted. As children, we appreciated the glamorous side of things. We did not realize until later in life that we were missing a critical piece from Miss Charlene, her love.

Because Miss Charlene did not have kids of her own, she never quite understood what it took to raise children, which is why I never knew what would make her choose to be with a man who already had children.

She thought purchasing material things would do. But deep down within, I felt Miss Charlene was a showoff. She didn't buy us things because she loved us; she did things to keep up her image. People would look at us from the outside and think, "Oh, your step momma is so sweet, and you guys are blessed." Not knowing she could have cared less about either one of us and if she did we didn't feel it. The only person Miss Charlene seemed to love was daddy. And it showed. She never paid any attention to us; she never came to any of our school functions. When things bothered us, she showed little or no concern. I cannot recall a single time she told us she loved us, or even hugged us, throughout the entire time we lived with her. But when it came to daddy, she made sure she showered him with affection every day. I wondered why the love she felt for daddy didn't flow to his children. I wanted to ask her, but I sensed I would be brushed off or ignored. I felt nervous and uncomfortable, so I never asked. In her eyes, it was just she and my daddy. Not us.

I would often compare her to my biological Momma. They seemed to have a few things in common. Abandonment would be the first commonality. For someone who always bad-mouthed my Momma, she didn't do any better raising us. Truthfully, Miss Charlene was worse than Momma, in my opinion. She was supposed to be an example of what a Momma should be. As much as I resented my Momma, at least she had the decency to leave. I prefer someone to be in my life mentally and physically, not just materialistically. I've always heard that some people have motherly instincts, and some don't. Maybe this is why she could never conceive. God knew she had no business being a Momma in the first place.

Finally, after being faced with years of back and forth arguments, things went sour between Miss Charlene and me. The older I got, the more Miss Charlene and I would argue. It didn't improve either. When I became a teenager, the arguments turned into fights. Her specialty was nitpicking! She would complain about something whenever I had company. I used to tell daddy that I felt like she was trying to embarrass me, but he didn't believe me. I guess he was to "whipped" because, in his eyes, she could do no wrong. I began to feel like I was no longer his little princess, and she had taken my daddy from me. I would confide in her about personal things, and she would throw them back in my face anytime we argued. A birth Momma doesn't do that. Nothing I did was ever good enough for her. If I cleaned the kitchen, it wasn't clean enough. If I cleaned my room and it didn't meet her expectations, she would ransack it and make me clean it over again. I hated her for this. Most of our arguments happened when daddy wasn't around. So, when he came home, she would switch into love mode and act as if nothing happened. The aftermath of one particular altercation we had, I'll never forget.

During a heated argument, I said to her, "You aren't my Momma!" She retorted, "I'm glad I'm not your Momma cause you too black and too ugly to be my child anyway!" That night I cried myself to sleep. For years I struggled with feelings of insecurity because of the color of my skin. The hurt I felt was deep. She and I had discussed this particular insecurity before. Then she turned around and used it to hurt me. Adults never seem to realize the power in their words. To this day, I never forgot how she made me feel at the moment. I began to feel ugly all over again. The hate for my birth Momma returned, and all of a sudden, it was her fault.

Trap Bible 12:12 Easily Influenced

Commandment: Thou Shall Not Believe the Hype

Summer was finally here, my favorite time of year—no school, late nights, and even later mornings. I was not a morning person, so sleeping in was something I enjoyed. But this was a tough summer for us. My brother had accidentally shot his best friend in the stomach. The bullet traveled through his stomach and severed his spinal cord and paralyzed him from the waist down. That really messed my brother up for a minute, he told me they were on their way to fight some other niggas when it happened. They were in the car, all riled up and ready to scrap. But when they pulled up and got out of the car, things went left. Face to face with the opposing group, shots rang out.

Jarvis pulled the gun from out of his waistband and fired back. His best friend was in the crossfire, and he didn't even realize it until he heard moans. "Ahh," He turned slightly to the left, and saw his homie crouched down on the ground in the fetal position. A stray bullet from Jarvis' gun struck him. "Fuck!" And soon as he got hit, Jarvis fled the scene. He didn't have time to stop, or he would've gotten caught in the crossfire. When I think about it now, maybe it was God saving my brother from being killed that day. We were finally moving forward.

My 14th birthday was right around the corner. I never understood when grownups would say, "A young girl smelled herself." (Meaning she was probably having sex) But right before my 14th birthday, my body began to change. I was about 5 feet 4 inches with shiny dark skin; my hair was long and silky and cut in a mushroom bob style. I was short in stature with curves that accented the thickness of my newly developed breast and slowly spreading hips. I guess you could say I was what they called fine. I never felt pretty because of my complexion, but that would soon change.

The pool in our apartment complex was the place to be during the summer, and it was LIT! From the neighborhood boys that I went to school with, the D-boys who were a few years older than me. They all hung out at the pool to get a glimpse of us girls walking around with 2-piece bathing suits and developing bodies. Some of us much more developed than others.

My friend Stacy and I were the same age, but she was more mature than me physically and mentally. My daddy used to say she was too fast for me because she was very popular with the boys and didn't have a lot of supervision at home. Stacy had a pecan brown complexion, and her hair was a thick Jehri curl style. Her shape envied by most girls our age, with legs that were sexy and bowed. Stacy was popular and pretty. All the boys admired her. To put the icing on the cake, she and her mom acted more like sisters or roommates. I respected their relationship. I often wished Miss Charlene, and I could be cool like them to some extent.

Stacy didn't have a curfew, and she pretty much came and went as she pleased. She knew how to drive, so she would often use her mom's, Carla car whenever Carla wanted privacy.

Carla was cool and funny, she was built like a stallion, as the men would say. Thick in all the right places, with long, toned legs. She kept her hair very short and always dressed in slacks and a collared shirt. Her breast was always pressed down in her shirt by way of sports bras, although chest compression didn't help much. You still knew they were there. Carla wore no makeup and often had a stern look on her face. Miss Charlene used to say she was a "bull dagger." Although I never believed her because I never knew you could have children and still be gay.

One day, my friend Niecy saw her and another lady, we all knew as her best friend, naked in bed. Back then, being gay or a bull dagger, as Miss Charlene would say, was not as accepted as it is now.

All the grownups in our neighborhood all knew Ms. Carla was gay, and Stacy would often get teased, sometimes even being called gay herself. I think she wanted to prove she wasn't gay.

Because out of the three of us, she was the first one to have sex.

As crazy as it sounds, I always thought it would be Niecy. Her mom was so mean and strict; she rarely came outside at all. Niecy was my best friend. She was more my speed. I think we were both curious about sex, but Niecy more so than me. We used to tell each other everything. I felt terrible for the things her mom would do to her. A busted lip, black eye, or large bruises were hard to cover up on her high yellow complexion. Niecy had long, naturally curly hair and the biggest booty you ever saw on a 14-year-old girl! Her shape was that of a grown woman. Niecy was very promiscuous. She would tongue kiss with boys, and get fingered fucked. I'd get all the juicy details about getting her cherry popped. Niecy always had this sexual demeanor about her. She was like some hot Mamacita you'd see in a Latin movie. By now, both of my friends were having sex, and I was more curious than ever. But none of the guys in my neighborhood were looking at me, mostly because of my brother. And the other part was I didn't think I was as cute or developed as the other girls in the neighborhood.

I remember this boy named Jacque, who was a friend of my brothers, told me if I let him suck my titties, they would grow. My crazy-ass believed him, so I let him suck my titties one day after school. Sucking my titties hurt! That nigga just about pulled my nipple off. I was thinking to myself. "This can't be how it is supposed to feel. Oh my fucking goodness, ouch dammit!" I screamed. "Just never mind!" They didn't grow, and still, to this day, I hate getting my titties sucked. I think he jinxed me.

In the summer of my 9th-grade year, a month before my 14th birthday, I succumbed to the peer pressure. Rod had just moved into the apartment complex. We were both the same age but went to different schools. He was cute, nicely built, and dressed in the latest styles. He was so arrogant a lot of girls liked him, and he knew it. We would all make our way to the basketball court. He had this walk that was so sexy. I had a thing for bow legs, and his legs were just the way I liked it.

I wasn't allowed to talk to boys on the phone yet, but I would always sneak and talk to him. I liked him, even though he could be an asshole. I remember him blatantly telling me one night on the phone that he was going to be my first. I was like, "Boy, you got me bent. No, you're not!" I giggled. He was like, "Okay, we will see." He had so much confidence. He acted as if he had heard girls tell him no a dozen times before only to give in. Because he had older brothers and sisters, he was mature for his age.

On this particular day after school, Rod was standing on the porch as I walked by. He usually got home before us and would stand outside and wait for our bus to come. My brother Jarvis played football, so he usually stayed for practice. We got off the bus, everybody laughed and talked about the upcoming rap battle between Big Man and white boy Travis. That shit was epic. I looked ahead, and I could see some of the guys had stopped to talk to Rod. Neicy and I always walked home together. My stop was last. As we got closer, Stacy said, "There's your boyfriend, Tameka."

I laughed and said, "Girl, I don't like him." I always said that even though I liked him. I think it was a way to protect myself if he said he didn't like me. Then it wouldn't hurt as much. As we walked by, we all said: "Hey Rod.'" And just as I was about to pass by, he shoved me and ran back towards his front door. I fell for it and ran after him. I attempted to get my lick back, and he ran right into his house and left the door open behind him. I thought his mom was home. I stopped at the entrance and said, "You better run with your scary self!" He came up front grinning. He said, "You're the one scared and talking all that mess from over there." I looked around curiously and said, "Yeah, because I don't want your Momma to hear me beating your ass!" He cocked his head to the side, looking at me with those sexy eyes and said, "Girl, my mama ain't even here." He continued to taunt me from inside. I ran up to him and hit him. We started to wrestle playfully. He pushed the door close and leaned me against the door and started kissing me. Now, we were pressed up against the door grinding and kissing, and I could feel his nature rise. It was so hard!

Still kissing, he slowly began walking back towards his room. At that moment, all I could think about was how he told me he would be my first. He laid me back onto his bed, and we continued to kiss and grind for what seemed like forever. His hand started to move up my jean skirt, and he began to play with my pussy until my panties became wet. He then slipped them to the side and put his finger inside of me, slowly moving his finger in and out. I could tell that I liked it because my hips started to roll with every movement of his finger. He then unbuckled his pants and slowly pushed himself inside of me. As soon as he got inside of me, it was over! I didn't know what to expect, but it was nothing like Stacy and Neicy had described. The thrill was gone instantly! I thought my first time would be painful, and I would bleed like a slaughtered pig! At least that was what Neicy said would happen.

I wish I had waited to experience sex. My first sexual experience, or lack thereof, left me perplexed. Before I had sex, it was tough having to pretend I was doing it. And then, when I finally "did it," it was tough to pretend that I hadn't. But at that point, it was too late. And one thing about Virginity, once it's gone, you'll never get it back.

To make matters worse, like most young and misguided girls my age, we tend to fall for the player type. So after we "fucked," of course, it was customary for him to get ghost. In an instant, I had experienced my first heartbreak. Rod started to date one of my cousins. What a bitch move! Boy, regret took over my psyche. I wouldn't even consider sex again for a whole year. But this time, it would be with my first love, Terry.

Trap Bible 13:13 A House Divided

Commandment: Thou Shall Love Through Pain

"The God of imagination lived in fairytales. And the best fairytales made you fall in love" (Diriye Osman). When I was living between homes is when I met my first love, Terry. He was not only the finest boy in Caravan; he was a top contender. He wasn't tall for a guy, and he stood a little over 5'6" inches. A few inches taller than me. He was medium built with Hershey kissed chocolate skin. He had the softest, thickest hair that he kept cut low to bring out his waves that would make you "see" sick. He had the longest eyelashes I'd ever seen on a boy, which made his eyes seem deep and dreamy. This boy was fine, and I wanted him. I like everything about him from how he talked, with that slow southern drawl, to the way he'd cracked a half-smile when he looked at me and revealed his shiny gold teeth.

How he would ever be attracted to me, I had no idea. I was smitten.

He had an easy-going personality and charm. He won over all the girls. He definitely wouldn't notice me; I was four years younger than him just entering 10th grade. He was used to dating girls that were much older with their apartments. That was the norm back then; girls would get pregnant have a baby and get approved for government housing.

After waiting two years to get subsidized housing, my Aunt Trina moved into her apartment in Caravan, which was a lot easier since she'd now had a baby, my *lil* cousin Pooh. Aunt Trina's house was the place to be on weekends, but not without a little strife. See, Aunt Trina was the bomb in more ways than one. She was tall and whip-thin with just the right amount of curves. Aunt Trina was super cute. She had a smooth brown complexion. A pair of arched eyebrows looked down on sweeping eyelashes. A set of dazzling white teeth gleamed when she smiled. But that mouth though! That mouth was something else. Man, this girl would curse you out like a sailor and out drink a grown man.

She was a straight firecracker. "No Trouble Trina" was her nickname. If she thought it, she said it, not giving one single fuck of how it came out or who she offended. And she had her share of niggas from all sides of town and different complexes who didn't fuck with each other. She was crazy, funny, and loud. So staying at her house on weekends, although it came with a lot, was so much fun. It was an escape from my everyday life.

As if her world and reputation couldn't get more complicated, Aunt Trina became a central part of an entire war rival between Caravan and Pottsburg. Two of the most notorious complexes in the hood. The hood always had drama and beef between someone or about something. Aunt Trina was in the mix when a group of ruthless, cocky mean ass niggas wrecked Club Mardi Gras. Come to find out, they tore the club up all because one of the niggas from Pottsburg found out that Aunt Trina was creepin' with a Caravan nigga. And they didn't play that mixing shit. Either you were on one side or the other. Ain't no playing the fields in the hood. As a result, not only did people's houses and cars get shot up, but people got hurt too. Luckily nobody got killed because that went on for what seemed like years.

To this day, that incident was known as one of the biggest rivalries in Jacksonville. But that was unknown to me, at least until I started coming around more regularly. Hell, all I wanted to do at that time was visit so I could get away from the drama that surrounded Miss Charlene's coldhearted ass, and so that I could see Terry. As far as I was concerned, that beef shit ain't have a lick to do with me. And I wanted to keep it that way.

When I couldn't get over to Aunt Trina's, my Aunt Janie's house would have to do. My Aunt Janie was my cousin, but because she was so much older, I called her auntie. She had four girls and two boys, and she had taken in my cousin Rina. Her two youngest girls,

Taryn and Serenity, and I were close. Rina and I weren't as close back then because she was the youngest, so I often ignored her. But eventually, she and I would become pillars in each other's lives. Rina was my first cousin on my mama side. My mom and her mom were sisters; both strung out on drugs. Aunt Regina had three kids that she wasn't raising just like Lou. Rina was the oldest, Rod, and TJ. Lou had a total of four sisters; one of them was bat shit crazy and would walk up and down the street butt naked. The other three hooked on drugs. I wanted nothing to do with this family. That's why I think I ignored Rina so much when we were kids. She reminded me of a piece of myself that I tried so hard to forget.

At this point in my life, I'd disassociated myself with this side of my family so much so that I didn't even acknowledge them. In my eyes, they didn't exist even down to Lou. I didn't even call her Momma anymore. I usually addressed her as "that lady" or Lou. She had been out of my life for over ten years now. My

Momma stayed in and out of prison, hooked on heroin. She didn't deserve to be called Momma. Momma's don't abandon their children. I hated her, and I hated her family too.

But in true Tameka fashion, I did my best to temporarily suppress my anger, and ignore the void in my life, by fixating my thoughts on Terry. I couldn't wait to get back to Caravan so that I could see him again. I imagined a life with him, and a non-dysfunctional family of our own. Wishful thinking.

Trap Bible 14:14 Scorned

Commandment: Thou Shall Not Blame Me

My family was like rotting teeth. All crown and no filling. How can a whole family of sisters be hooked on drugs? I would often ask myself. They did everything together except raise their kids. It was like when one got hooked on drugs, and another would persuade the other to try it. This family was full of crooks and drug addicts.

The crimes of fraud, check fraud, credit card fraud, and forgery, whatever it took to get that next hit is how they fed their addiction. I was embarrassed to be a part of them. I had so much hate and resentment for Lou by now that I wished she was dead. I remember the day I started saying she died. We were eating dinner as we watched the six o'clock news. "Police have been called to the scene of the Econo Lodge on Philips Highway and Emerson where one person was found dead of an apparent drug overdose. Police have arrested one other person, Lucille Tiggs, who was with the deceased at the time of death." The reporter continued. Momma's charges were: possession of a controlled substance, drug paraphernalia, and an outstanding warrant. As I took another bite of food, I looked up at the TV and there she was. Her mug shot was staring me straight in the face.

The sound of the journalist's voice faded. I stared at the TV in shock, and she continued, "Channel 4 News has learned that the suspect has a long criminal history. The suspect will appear in court tomorrow to see if felony or murder charges are attached. We will keep you posted." There was complete silence. I couldn't believe what I heard and saw. After not seeing her all these years, I was able to see her face on the television screen. "A fucking baser" is what I thought to myself. I was more disgusted than ever. My dad looked just as shocked as I did seeing her on TV. Miss Charlene couldn't let the moment pass without saying something.

"You have to be careful who you have *chiren* with." She said it as if we were a product of this shit. My daddy quickly said, "My *chiren* good as long as I got breathe in my body, I'm gonna make sure of that." I felt my stomach tighten and looked at Miss Charlene. I hated that Bitch too, and she always had something to say. I can't begin to tell you how much anger and resentment I felt at that moment. It was on that day I decided she was dead to me too. I had no Momma! Not Miss Charlene, not Lou! NOBODY! I made myself a promise that day that whenever I became a Momma, I would be better than both of my parents, and that was a promise I intended to keep!

Trap Bible 15:15 Ballistic Chicks

*Commandment: Thou Shall Not F*S% With Me*

Niecy slapped her Momma with an open hand across the face. It rocked her, she took a step back and then steadied herself, blinking her eyes and staring at Niecy. She snatched a hand full of Niecy's hair, returned the favor, and slapped the shit out of Niecy.

The fighting between Niecy and her Momma had gotten bad. Niecy eventually moved with her Grandmomma on the Northside of town. It was difficult for us to see each other after she moved.

I finally entered high school. My friend Stacy was a different beast than Niecy. She had made a name for herself. She was very popular with boys and girls. They bowed down to her, so to speak as if she was the Queen. Not me, I ain't never been a weak bitch and wasn't going to start! Stacy knew I didn't go out like that from the many fights she and I had gotten into over the past few years. Our relationship wasn't the same. We started to drift apart. I wasn't gonna do two things, and that would be kissing her ass or be her, yes, man. I no longer fit into her circle. It didn't matter to me; I had a new friend, Kira.

Ironically, Kira was seeing Stacy's ex-boyfriend, Thomas. That shit didn't fly with Stacy, and now she wanted to fight me. Or so she thought! Stacy wanted none of me, but I let her believe whatever she wanted! See, I learned how to fight when I lived with my Grandmomma. Shit, I lived in a house with ten people. You had to stay in survivor mode! You had to line that shit up, or you got dragged! There were plenty of days when Aunt Trina drug my ass! So, I had to learn quickly and stay ready, so I wouldn't have to get ready. In other words, I had to learn how to fight, to keep from getting my ass whooped every day.

I might have been small in size, but I had heart. I wasn't scared of nobody! I didn't care what size you were; you could get it on sight! I didn't believe in fighting fair either, I always picked up something, whether it was a stick, a brick, a bottle even a hammer. If I could get my hands on something, you can best believe I was gone fuck you up with it. Period!

My dad always told me that I had so much anger built up, and I needed to learn how to control my temper because my bad temper was going to get me in big trouble one day. Old folks would say, "Warning comes before destruction." Well, they also said a "Hardhead made a soft behind." And life would later show me how true those statements would be.

I sat on the porch and talked with Bobby one day after school when Stacy and two of her friends rode by and yelled out, "Bitch!" as they drove off. It took me by surprise because I didn't know any of the girls with her. But I did see that they probably went to Raines High School with her. Raines was the most popular school in the city. So popular, the name of the school was dropped in a hit song. "Chill in the Ville," by the 69

Boyz was the title of the song, I think. I went to Englewood High School; it was the school for my neighborhood district.

Everybody wanted to attend Raines High School! I wanted to attend Raines high school too, but my Momma wouldn't let me. Raines was one of the most popular high schools in the city. And to be one of the elite, you had to know how to dress, because this school was a fashion show.

The bell rang at 2:40 pm to release the student body at Raines High School. On Friday's when the bell rang everybody would hang out in Raines parking lot whether you went to school there or not. We would skip our last period class on Fridays to ride through the parking lot. Raines was lit! We'd go to Raines because all the dope boys either went there or hung out there. We were new faces from the south side, so we stood out amongst the regular faces. And by this time, I was full of confidence. I don't know where the confidence came from because Miss Charlene wasn't the type to build me up. I mean, my daddy used to tell me I was beautiful all the time, but that's what all daddies told their daughters.

Nonetheless, I had grown into myself, hell, I was borderline conceited. I was brown skin, cute, with long hair that I kept stacked. My signature hairstyle was a bob, long on one side short on the other side. I was thick in the waist with a fat ass. I was fine, and I knew it!

I had taken Drivers Education over the summer. So by the time school started, I could drive, and my dad would let me use the car for a few hours on the weekends. You couldn't tell me nothing, riding around in our burgundy Camry with the shiny gold rims. Anyways, after hearing her yell "Bitch," I kinda looked and laughed because I knew for sure she had beef now after seeing me and Kira at Englewood and

Wolfson's Homecoming game with Thomas Friday night.

When Stacy returned to the apartment complex, she decided to stop and asked me what I said. She got out of her car, as I stood on my front porch. She started walking toward me with her friends in tow.

It was hot outside, and there was no breeze at all. As soon as she got within arm's reach, the battle began. I punched her in the face. Stacy clawed at me, and I kept pounding her in the eye. Stacy pulled at my hair, and I hit her again in the eye.

Stacy screamed so loud the entire complex could hear her scream. Blood oozed down her face. We were fighting like two grown women. We were going so hard that my stepmom heard the commotion outside and came out to attempt to break us apart. But I was not letting go of Stacy, who tried her best to get away from me.

There was a mop in the corner of Mrs. Margaret's front porch, and I tried to get my hands on it. I was gonna beat the living shit out of that whore! And that's just what I did! I fucked her up that day. Stacy shrieked in pain, grasping the gaping wound where her eye was, and in a frenzy, she grabbed at my right arm, but I weaved out of her reach and twisted her arm 720 degrees. And with a sickening, cracking noise, I knew. That did it. The bitch was through dealing! She was screaming in so much pain, and her little scary-ass friends helped her get to her car. She was not looking back. She wore an ass whipping so bad she had to lie and say Bobby and my step momma jumped in the fight, which was a lie! I just fucked her up—point-blank.

Her mom came to our apartment and tried to start an argument with Bobby about Stacy, but we stopped her from trying to blame us. It wasn't long before Stacy moved, and I didn't see her to until a couple of years later. It was put up or shut up, and Stacy had to shut the fuck up and move!

Trap Bible 16:16 Uncharted Territory

Commandment: Thou Shall Not Play with Fire

Since I was driving now, I would ride over to my Aunt's Trina's house on Saturdays when I could get the car. After seeing me a few times, Terry had finally decided to say something to me. It wasn't what I was expecting, but I was just happy he was talking to me. "Why, you ain't tell me you was a *jit*?" Jit is slang for an underage person.

I frowned at him. "Huh?" I acted like I didn't know what he was saying. "What you talking about?" I replied. "You heard me," he said. "I ain't know you was nothing but fifteen-years-old."

I smiled. "Oh yeah? Well, I am. Who told you that, my auntie?" He licked his lips. "Yeah, she told all us you off-limits." She said, "Your daddy crazy, and he will kill all us up in this bitch."

I shrugged like that shit ain't matter. "Oh my God, she talks too much." I tried to ease his mind. I said, "No, he not." I laughed flirtatiously and asked, "So you scared of my daddy?" I looked him straight in the eyes. "Ain't you from Caravan? Ain't you supposed to be fearless?"

I stood with one of my hands on my hips, waiting for a reply. Terry shook his head, and I didn't know if that was a no, or if he was shaking his head because he was checking out my fine ass. "I can't tell," I said. I could tell he was feeling my *lil* young ass cuz as I was walking away I heard him tell his friend Fat Daddy, "She gone make a nigga rob the cradle with her *lil* fine ass."

He reached in front of his pants and grabbed his dick that was rising to the occasion. "*Oh shit*!" I said to myself, as I was closing the front door to Aunt Trina's apartment.

A Trap Girls Bible

Trap Bible 17:17 Grown Man

Commandment: Thou Shall Not Take Him From Me

Terry and I were exactly four years apart. We shared the same birthday. Aunt Trina kept a house full of company, and the older guys always tried to get with me. But she was always cock blocking. *(A term used in the hood. Is the action of preventing someone (usually a man) from having sex by intentionally or unintentionally stopping (blocking) someone else from reaching its intended destination)* "Uhmmm . . . gone in the back with Pooh." Is what she would say. "Ya'll niggas ain't finna make my brother kill me.

Terry was different from the rest of the guys. He was real laid back, very respectful. You could tell he was smart when he wasn't with his homeboys because he spoke differently. Aunt Trina and I were close. I could tell her anything, and it would stay between us, and that has not changed.

I told her how much I liked Terry, and she wasn't at all surprised. "I knew you liked that lil' ugly nigga. I see the way y'all look at each other when you come over here. Ya' ass probably come over here all the time so that you can see his ass anyway." I giggled because it was true. "Uh-huh, I know…yo' lil' hot ass ain't gotta tell me, cause' I already know. But I like Lil Terry. He a good dude as far as I know." She would let him come over when I was there, but she told us both if shit ever hit the fan, she would tell my dad she knew nothing about nothing. We pinky squared that I would take the fall if shit ever hit the fan.

Terry was worth whatever consequences I had to face. We were inseparable if we weren't on the phone, I was blowing up his pager. My code was 99, which was our birthday, September ninth. He used to come to pick me up from school in his **Pink and Blue Chevrolet Chevette**. I could hear the boom from the big box speaker he had in the back from my classroom. He was different from any boy I had met. He was a grown man, and I was his girl.

I shared everything with Terry. He was my confidante and non-judgmental. Terry was compassionate when I expressed my feelings about Miss Charlene, and that helped form an indisputable connection between us. When I said how I felt about Lou, he comprehended and nurtured those feelings. I didn't feel powerless after an honest sharing of what I had been through in life. He was becoming my best friend. Terry had similar family issues, so he understood me. Anytime, Miss Charlene and I would get into it, just talking to him would ease my mind. He promised he would take me away from my toxic environment soon. I hated that he would be leaving for the military soon, but after that Pottsburg and Caravan mess, he said he saw his life flash before his eyes and felt that joining the military would be for the best.

We talked about sex but not much because he never pressured me about it. I told him about the time I had sex with Rod, and he laughed at me. According to him, I was still a virgin because so much time had passed. I insisted I was not because I wanted to seem mature. Even though he never pressured me about sex, a part of me felt pressured because all of those older girls liked him and would stop at nothing to get him. They always had something to say about his *lil* girlfriend. I was a *lil* girl to them, but I had something they wanted, and I knew he wouldn't wait on me forever. So once again, I succumbed to the pressure.

It happened the day after my 16th birthday, which was also his 20th birthday. At the time, we felt it would be best to tell my dad he was 18. He arrived at my house at around six o'clock. The knock at the door had me nervous and excited. Nervous because I didn't know if my dad would allow me to go on a date with Terry and excited because I'd been looking forward to us hanging out. My dad answered the door. Terry stood there dressed, so fly, looking good as shit. I prayed my daddy wouldn't cut up too bad. I heard Terry say, "How you doing sir, is Tameka at home?" My dad looked him up and down, still standing in the doorway. "Yeah, who you say you is?" He smiled slightly, tilted his head, and said, "I'm her friend Terry, and I wanted to know if it would be ok to take her to the movies this evening?" Dad turned his back and left the door open. He didn't say a word to Terry about coming in. "Tameka!" He called my name like I stole something. "Your company here. You didn't mention going to the movies."

I shrugged and said, "I meant to ask you daddy but . ." He looked from Terry to me. "What time the movie over?" Terry looked at his watch and said, "It starts at seven and ends around nine." My dad told Terry, "Have her home by Eleven." He walked out of the room. Terry nodded. "Yes, sir." Terry grabbed my hand. "*Damn, daddy was stale as fuck with Terry,*" I thought to myself. But I was just happy he even let me go. "Love you, daddy," I yelled as I walked out the door.

We went to see the Denzel Washington movie **Mo' Betta Blues**, or at least it's beginning. Because thirty minutes into the film, we got up and left. Terry had made reservations at a hotel before picking me up. There was an adorable stuffed teddy bear, and fake rose placed on the bed when we entered. We had about an hour and a half left before I had to be home.

Terry immediately started kissing me, and his lips were soft as a ripened peach. He laid me down on the bed and began kissing my neck as his hand started to explore my body. Reaching his first destination, Terry began to caress my breast and unfastened my bra with ease and familiarity. Laying there with my breast exposed, he began to kiss them while gently pulling on my nipple. This feeling was not the same feeling I had when, *Jaque* did it, I thought. This feeling felt so good, and I could feel myself getting wet as he continued.

Moving from my breast, he slid his tongue down the middle of my stomach until he reached his final destination. Slowly removing my panties, he continued to kiss between my thighs while softly rubbing my clit. My body automatically assumed an arched position. With two fingers, he spread the lips of my vagina apart and started to lick me up and down as if he were licking an ice cream cone.

Stacy and Neicy had never shared this part of sex with me. I didn't know what he was doing, and I was slightly confused between feeling gross or this being the best feeling I ever felt! All I knew was, I liked it, and I didn't want him to stop. So, I grabbed his head and held it tight between my legs as he continued to devour me.

He paced himself and focused on my breast. Rubbing my breast while devouring me, and pinching them between his fingers had me rupture like a volcano. Slowly, he slid up my body and kissed me while removing his pants. I wanted him so bad I could feel the muscle in my pussy pulsating. When he was completely naked, he revealed he was not a little boy! I compared him to the first male penis I encountered, and Terry was hung! I mean it looked like it was halfway down his leg. He was all man, I thought to myself.

It took at least 10 minutes before he could insert his entire penis inside of me. Each time he attempted to penetrate deeper, I would slide back. It hurt so bad, and I initially felt like I was going to split in two and scream. He whispered in my ear, placing soft wet kisses on my face. "Stop running from me; I'm going to take it easy, I promise." With every move, he made he would be sure to kiss me and ask me if I was ok or if I wanted him to stop. But I didn't want him to stop. I'd now learned what it meant when they say, "The hurt felt good." Who knew pleasure and pain could coexist so well? He was so gentle with me, yet so forward. I just couldn't resist him. Whatever Rod' called himself doing to me sexually back then, didn't hold a candle to what I experienced with Terry.

But afterward, the bloodstains on the sheets showed I was no longer a virgin. My body ached, and I hardly had the strength to walk. Terry was nervous. I was too. "Shit, T! You can't go home walking like that. Your daddy will know what we've done." I practiced walking until the pain subsided, and I could walk as normal as possible before I got home. Terry got a kick outta that shit!

When I finally got home, Terry was like a scratched record in my head. I replayed the evening over and over again. I couldn't wait to have sex with Terry again. I wanted him to teach me everything. For the next few days, that night with Terry was the only thing on my mind. Terry was not like the boys at school. He was grown, and I felt grown-up whenever I was with him. I started to feel like guys my age were just too childish for me. The rapper Plies said it best, Terry "exposed me to real," and now, a lame nigga was something I wanted NOTHING to do with.

I couldn't get enough of him. Come to think about it, sex with Terry almost made me feel like I could semi resonate with Lou. All it took was one hit of him, to keep my ass coming back over and over again. I was overly eager, overly curious, and overly in "love" --- with the dick.

It took four more times after our first time having sex before I could take the dick without running from it. That practice walk was an inside joke for us, and we would laugh about it often.

Making love to me was not the only way Terry pleased me. He showered me with gifts. Terry would buy me jewelry, clothes, shoes whatever I needed. He made sure I was straight. He even taught me how to drive a stick shift. I stripped his clutch in the process, but I eventually got the hang of it.

Terry would be leaving for basic training in a couple of weeks, and I hated that he was leaving me. I knew it was for the best. We had talked about getting married after I graduated from high school and starting our own family. We promised each other that we wouldn't let time apart come between us.

Trap Bible 18:18 Trust Me

Commandment: Thou Shall Not Lose Trust in Me

Terry reported to Ft. Myers, Florida, after his basic training ended. We would write to each other all the time. But Terry wanted a letter every day, and when he didn't receive one, he became suspicious. He wanted to know what kept me so busy that I couldn't write to him. I would write and tell him repeatedly; I wasn't doing anything with other boys. I tried my best to reassure him, but his distrust in me, coupled with our long-distance love affair, quickly placed a strain on our relationship. Terry was at his breaking point. He wanted to end our relationship because he was always worried about me with other guys.

Call it naive or unknowledgeable, but I always thought people enlisted in the military to have a better life and be better. But it did just the opposite for Terry. He would write about his time on the military base and all the people he came across. To my surprise, a lot of guys in his platoon were coke heads. I kept wondering why every letter he sent seemed to reference coke in some capacity, but I just attributed it to him, giving it to me raw, telling me every little thing he was experiencing at the time. Shows how much I know, cause' I thought they did random drug testing in the military. He knew how I felt about drugs, after seeing what it did to Lou and my aunts. Even some of his people too. So, I couldn't understand why the hell he kept bringing it up? I hated crack, coke, heroin all of it! I didn't consider weed as a drug because I would smell it coming from my parent's room. But that's neither here nor there.

Over the next few weeks, Terry and I wouldn't talk as much. I chalked it up to him being busy and working, and so I didn't think much of it. I knew he would be coming home on a weekend pass soon, and I was looking forward to that. We hadn't had sex in a while, and my *lil* hot ass was ready.

Trap Bible 19:19 Fake Friend

Commandment: Thou Shall Not Dishonor the G-Code

Knock, knock, "Who is it?" I asked, "It's Rashad is Jay home?" I didn't even acknowledge the voice on the other side of the door instead .... "Jarvis!" I screamed, "Somebody at the door for you." He hollered back, "Let him in stupid. I'm coming." I stomped toward the door, mumbling, "You stupid. . . and my name ain't Benson, and you better be glad I'm feeling nice today with your black ass!" We always argued. It was a sign of affection.

When I opened the door, the first thing that caught my attention was a beautiful pair of light brown eyes. I had to catch my breath. I was in a temporary trance. When I came to, I said, "Come in; Jarvis is in the back. He'll be out in a minute." He was like no other boy I had ever seen before. I didn't even know who he was, but there was just something about him that caught my attention. He had naturally curly hair that he wore in a

'High top Fade.' His eyes sparkled with dark chocolate skin and a smile that showed a few extra teeth. "*Who was he? I had never seen him before. He must not be from around here.*" I thought. I found out he recently moved to the neighborhood from the Hilltop projects. He went to Raines, but once he moved, he would have to catch two buses to Raines High School. I must have caught his eye too because as he sat on the couch waiting on my brother, I noticed him staring at me.

I discovered his name was Rashad. Rashad was considered a bad boy. Not that Terry was a saint, but you could tell the difference. Some people do bad things, but that doesn't define who they are; it describes what they did. Then there are people whose character says, "I am trouble, and I look for trouble." Rashad had trouble written all over him. Already a part of the juvenile delinquent system for stealing a car, it's no wonder he and Jarvis were friends. Now almost 18, Jarvis had started to follow in my dad's footsteps. He was always into something. Jay was a hustler; his skills were making money, but most important, Jay knew how to save it. He never robbed anybody and didn't respect niggas who chose that route. My brother could fight, and he was known for knocking niggas out. He had a one-hitter quitter, and you were out cold. That was Jarvis, a real live Debo like that crazy ass character in the movie "Friday."

Rashad and Jarvis had gotten pretty close, and he was always at our house. He knew I had a boyfriend in the military because he would see us together when Terry was home. That didn't stop him from trying to talk to me. He had transferred from Raines to Englewood, so we attended the same school. Jarvis went to University Christian on a football scholarship. I always had a feeling that Rashad liked me. The intense stares, looking me up and down and licking his lips when he saw me, the whole nine. I just didn't know how far he would go to get with me.

My last year of high school things with Terry and I started to change. Something was different with him, I didn't quite know what it was, but I could see the change in his personality. We went form spending our weekends together whenever he was home to him, not telling me he was in town on some occasions.

"Where you been, cuz you ain't been at your Momma house. I asked out of curiosity. "I've been calling there all weekend, Terry," I said. "Why the fuck you ain't answer my page?" This argument became the norm for us. I always felt like he would eventually get an older girl with an apartment, and not wanting to lose him, I felt like I needed to be on my own. The only way to accomplish that was to get pregnant. As crazy as it was, at 16 years old, Terry and I started trying to get pregnant. I wanted a baby so bad, and I told myself that I would never leave my child if I ever had one. My child would always know that I loved him or her with my whole heart, and he or she would love me just as much, something I've longed for my entire life. I would be a better Momma than both of my trifling parents. They would see.

I was happy to be a senior and ready to finish high school. I always felt like I was too mature to be mixed up in high school flings. The guys were like *lil* boys to me. A few of the guys at school, I would call my *lil* boyfriend, but it was just for fun. Rashad and I had gotten cool since he transferred to Englewood. He would walk me to my classes, and I even let him share my locker. He was acting as if he was the overprotective brother at first. Rashad hated my friends calling him one of my *lil* boyfriends. He would always say, "I got your *lil* boy" or reference that he thought he could do better than Terry like, "I bet I make more money than your boyfriend' or "Ya' lil nigga will never be this fly." He was always comparing himself to Terry, but to me, there was no comparison. I would always tell Rashad that Terry set the bar too high for him or any of these guys at school.

Terry would send me money for things I needed, and when he would come home, he would always buy me something. Terry had the material and sexual things on lock as far as I was concerned. Shit, once you date a guy with a car, you will never see a guy riding a bike again. Once you date a nigga with money, a broke one will never impress you. That was my mindset. But Rashad was persistent, and being a badass meant doing whatever it would take to get what he wanted, and his want was me.

One day after school, Rashad stopped by the house to show off in a car he had stolen. I could hear the music blasting from the speakers from inside the house. The group **Geto Boyz,** the song **"My Mind Playing Tricks on Me,"** was sounding off. That was my shit! As I looked out my window to see who had pulled up, I didn't recognize the car. I walked to the front door, and there Rashad was just about to ring the doorbell. "What you want, Rashad, Jay ain't home. Who car you done stole, and what?" Before I could get another word, he said, "Damn girl, slow down, why you questioning me like that, you act like you my old lady or something. and maybe I didn't come to see Jay ole smart mouth, ass girl." I rolled my eyes, "Whatever Rashad," I said.

"What you want then?" He wasn't going for it. "Quit playing Meka, you know a nigga like you, when are you gone let me take you out." I was not feeling this. "Oh my God, here we go again." I *giggled* and then said, "Rashad, you know I got a boyfriend, and besides, I told you Ya'll *lil* boys at school couldn't do nothing for me." He wasn't hearing me. "What your man got to do with me, and I told you, I ain't them niggas at school, and I got ya *lil* boy right here too." As he grabbed the front of his pants. "Ugh, you so nasty, bye Rashad, I'll tell Jay you came by." He walked away and said, "Alright, do that, I'm gonna show you, though, you gonna see." He sped off.

The next day Rashad and two of his friends robbed a jewelry store off of Hendricks Ave. Rashad being the mastermind, kept most of it while the other two divided what was left. No one at school knew Rashad had done this, we all thought he was selling drugs or something.

Almost every day for the next several weeks, I had a new piece of jewelry left inside the locker Rashad, and I shared. I had big diamond rings, coin rings, diamond pendants, necklaces, tennis bracelets, Turkish ropes with the bracelets to match. I had so much jewelry; both of my hands had two rings on them. At seventeen, I was walking the halls of high school with thousands of dollars' worth of jewelry on not knowing they were stolen goods.

There is an old saying, *"I wish I knew then what I know now."* Because I didn't have a clue, I was impressed, Rashad had stepped up his game, and I was ready to play. You couldn't tell me nothing, with my bamboo earrings, jean shorts, leather in the front and my floral printed shirt. I was feeling myself, and I had the dope girl look down packed. Rashad was about to give Terry some severe competition, so I thought.

One of the boys Rashad robbed the jewelry store with tried to pawn some of the jewelry. Instead, he got arrested. Not wanting to take the fall himself, he told on Rashad. They confiscated most of my jewelry. I did keep a few things I had at home but very little. The detectives told me that if I kept anything, I would be an accessory. Rashad was almost eighteen-years-old. The Judge sentenced him to ten years as an adult. That was the last time I saw him. He wrote often and tried to keep in touch, but as time went on, my desire to write decreased.

Trap Bible 20:20 Failure

Commandment: Thou Shall Not Switch Sides

Over the next couple of months, things with Terry and I were hit or miss whenever he came home. Some weekends were good, and some weekends we couldn't stand to be around each other. He had changed so much over the last year. We both had. I was changing because I was pregnant with our son, but he for an entirely different reason. He had become someone I didn't even know or never knew. He had gone from being a cool, calm, and collective man to being paranoid about everything! Terry would believe people were watching him or following him. The frequent mood swings were severe. He'd be cool one minute, and angry as fuck the next.

To make matters worse, one night, we were chilling at the Motel 8, when for some strange reason, Terry kept, peeping from behind the curtains out of the window. He looked out of that window about fifty times. I yelled at him, "Terry, like what is wrong with you?" I looked at him questionably. "Who the hell are you looking for?" He sank on the bed, "Shhhh. . . be quiet. They coming, they coming." He whispered. His pupils were dilated and red. His eyes bulged as if he had seen a ghost. "Who coming?" I jumped up. "What are you talking about, Terry?" He lowered his body from in front of the window. "Shhhh. . . he said again. "Hush for what!" I shouted, what the hell is going on?" The anger alone in my voice must have made him snap out of the trance. He tried to play that shit off by laughing. But I could see; clearly, he wasn't playing, and if he had been, it was a stupid joke. I remember seeing that look in his eyes once before, and I wouldn't say I liked it. I moved over to where he was sitting on the bed, and I said as calmly as I could, "I don't know what's wrong with you, but you are tripping', and I want you to take me home now." I tried to remain calm because I didn't know which way his mood would swing. He acted as if he didn't hear me. So, I wasn't playing nice anymore. "You are acting weird again, and I ain't with that shit! So, as soon as I get done peeing, I'm gonna be ready to go!" At seven months pregnant, it seemed as if I had to pee every ten minutes. I was pissed off! I didn't know why he was acting the way that he was.

When I was going to the bathroom, I saw a twenty-dollar bill on the counter. I picked the twenty-dollar bill up and placed it into my pocket. I noticed it had some white powder on it. "What the fuck is this?" I said to myself. I know this ain't what I think it is. It can't be. He wouldn't. We were about to have a son, and Terry hated coke heads and crack heads just as much as I did. All these thoughts ran through my mind as I stood in disbelief. If nobody knew how I felt about drug addicts, Terry most definitely knew! He knew I did not associate with my entire family because they were all addicts. Terry knew everything! He knew my Momma's history with drugs and what drugs had done to destroy my family. How could this be happening to me? How could he do this to our son? I thought his surroundings would be better going into the Army. Terry went in one way and came out another way.

After that night in the hotel, things would never be the same between us. He promised he would stop, but I guess he couldn't. He was too far gone—another weak-minded drug addict just like Lou. Lou had also abandoned her sons and me too. I started to feel as if everyone I cared for or loved would eventually end up leaving me. First daddy, then Momma, Rashad, was gone and now Terry. All those losses at such an early age changed me. It made me not want to love anyone fearing I would lose them too. I became cold and hard. I started not to care about losing people in my life. I conditioned my mind to never love anybody again to the point that it would affect me if they left. If they left, they left, I wouldn't care. It was gonna be about me; this is what life had made me. Unloving. Later, Terry failed a drug test discharging him from the Army. How the fuck you leave to escape a life of drugs and crime, just to come back home a coke head? Where they do that at my nigga!?

Trap Bible 21:21 Hurting

Commandment: Thou Shall Never Put Thy Trust in a F*&% Nigga

Life had dealt me an unlucky hand, and I played it the best I could. I had two months left in my pregnancy, and I find out that the daddy of my child is a fucking coke head. I was beginning to think this was some kind of curse. Terry was no longer the man that left a year ago.

The night I went into labor, I was reluctant to page him. My fingers trembled over the phone keys as I pressed the code #99-911. The code indicated I was about to have our baby. He immediately called back. "Hey, I'm on my way. I'mma bring your Aunt Trina with me cuz I know yo' daddy gonna be tripping." I hung up in disgust. I couldn't fathom him being near my child or me. The thought of him being on drugs was a total turn off. Just knowing my baby's daddy was on drugs infuriated me. Having him near me or my child was a decision I struggled to make in peace.

Despite my daddy and step-mother Miss Charlene being with me at the hospital, the loneliness I felt was like a vice on my heart, squeezing with just enough pressure to be a constant pain. My family and friends felt like paper chains in the rain and the sky holding nothing but the promise of more storms, and life was lonely. Other girls my age were planning to attend the Senior "PROM." Yet, there I was having a baby, and out of anger and the emotional desire to have my baby's daddy there for me, Terry was present. I let my inhibitions go, at least for a brief moment.

All I desired was a hand to hold or an arm about my shoulders insincerity, none manifested. Instead, the world became cold and empty, a slow poison for my soul.

I was born to be loved and nurtured, and it wasn't to be. It was then that I wished I could melt in the rain like snow, fade away, anything to stop the ever-present pain of loneliness. But my son needed me. The pure fight in me would not allow loneliness to overcome the lioness in motherhood.

My daddy hated Terry, and he did not hide it. Raw anger shot through him! He was one second away from giving Terry his first and last unadulterated ass-whipping. A whipping he would never forget! "Nigga, didn't I tell you to stay away from my daughter? You must take me for a joke!" He charged at Terry, fists flailing. Terry jumped back. Miss Charlene jumped between them.

Miss Charlene wasn't much help in calming my dad down. Hell, he almost shoved her out of the way but paused before he reacted. I was already in pain, physically and mentally, at this moment, but what pissed me off further was not the division between Terry and my dad. But instead, it was Miss Charlene's constant rejection of anything I said or did. As usual, she chose to throw the blame in a fucked up shady way, instead of understanding that pregnancy was foreign to me.

I didn't need her reminding my daddy that I made an adult decision to have sex. Miss Charlene took it to the hood level that only she could articulate. "Rome stop, you trying to fight this boy when your daughter laid up with him? It ain't just his fault!" She pulled daddy back as he simmered. "I told you she was smelling herself. You ain't wanna hear me!"

Smelling yourself was a term black folks used when they thought a young girl was having sex.

With all the commotion in the room and daddy trying to get to Terry, my contractions became harder and harder. Thank God because my contractions were the only thing that stopped daddy from going after Terry. Seeing me in pain quickly changed his mind. Daddy and Miss Charlene went to the waiting room to calm down while Aunt Trina and Terry stayed with me. Trina was always clowning, so it was comforting to have her with me. Terry couldn't even look me in the eyes because he knew how disgusted I was with him. He had done everything he could imagine to get me back except stop snorting coke! I lost all respect for him. Terry was used to me being mean throughout my pregnancy, but now I had become plain hateful and disrespectful. I held nothing back when I spoke to him. He was a coke head, a nothing ass, ain't' shit ass nigga who was never gonna see my child again if it was up to me.

Trina thought everything was funny as usual. Until I dug deep and found the meanest insults, I could think of to fire at him. I wanted him to hurt as he had hurt me. I guess I must have hit below the belt because all of a sudden, she stopped laughing and said, "Girl cut that shit out. It's too late for all that now. That's yo' baby daddy!" I looked at her hard and straight. "You got me fucked up; my baby don't have a daddy! Not a coke head, daddy. The hurt in his eyes when I said that gave me a feeling of pure satisfaction.

Shortly after, our son was born. Labor was scary and the most painful experience I'd had at that point. I was exhausted after the birth of my son. I fell asleep and slept for hours. When I woke up and opened my eyes, Terry was sitting down, holding our son. "Gimme my baby!" I said, still exhausted from labor and barely able to sit up. He said, "Meka, please. I promise! I won't hurt him—I," I interrupted abruptly, whatever he about to say. "I promise this will be the last time you hold my baby." He began to beg, "I 'ma stop, I swear; just give me a chance." Tears rolled down his face. "No!" I said, so cold and heartless. "You better take it all in while you can!"

That night he held Lil Terry for hours. It was as if he knew it would be the last time seeing him, or at least for years to come. Just like Momma, Terry let drugs destroy him and take him away from his only child. He tried to stop several times, but he couldn't do it. Neither would I! I wanted NO part of drugs. Not for my son or me. My decision had nothing to do with

Terry as a person. But Terry and drugs. I wouldn't do it with Terry ever again, and I meant that!

The Terry I knew had such a kind heart and sweet spirit. However, the cracks in my seemingly "Mr. Perfect" became too much to bear. I often wondered what would have been the outcome had I given him a second chance. Would he have stopped using drugs, or would I have become a crack head too? I guess that's something I will never know. Only God knows. As for me.

I was somebody's Momma. I had a baby boy that I instantly loved more than anything in the world. I made a promise to protect and love him, and never abandon him. He was my everything, and nothing would separate us. I had gone through so much, and I was barely eighteen-years-old. I guess God saw fit for me to endure what I did. Because without the rain, I would've never seen the fruits of my labor, my SON-shine, Terry Jr. I was now "mother earth," he represented my harvest, and I would water and nurture him.

During those early years of my life, I learned I was a warrior. I could raise a child, cook the food, clean the house, go to work, smile, and do it all with a broken heart. Talk about a heavy load, yet I made it look easy. I was broken on the inside and polished on the outside. But a **"TRAP"** life can easily break you down if you let it, and I refused to let anyone see me sweat, so finding ways to camouflage those shattered pieces was a skill I acquired and mastered early on.

Trap Bible 22:22 Living by the Sword

Commandment: Thou Shall Find Son-Shine in The Rain

With so many losses already, life still wasn't done. We lost my cousin Rod right after my 20th birthday. He was murdered execution-style along with his homeboy. Jarvis and Rod were always close, so that was difficult for Jay too. Even though Jay was older, Rod had seen more and jumped off the porch a long time before he did. My daddy even let Rod live with us a few times when Rod was between homes. He always looked out for a Sistah anytime he saw me, Cuz was getting money, and because of that, his family members and friends envied him.

Drugs and crime had brought so much dysfunction within the Tiggs family. "Why does this keep happening to us?" I said in disbelief. Not the people who he thought had his back. This couldn't be true; it just couldn't be, were the only words that would come out. If what I was hearing was true, this family was a lot worse then I imagined. I remember the day like it was yesterday, being at the funeral, sitting a few rows behind Rina, and seeing her cry out for her brother in agony. Watching her made me think about Jarvis and what if that had been him. The thought of losing Jay is something my heart couldn't take. It's been him and me our whole life, all we had was each other. My heart broke for Rina that day, I could only imagine what she was feeling, and we weren't even close. But that would soon change over the next few years.

I was now twenty-five with two kids. I thought I was doing okay for myself. I had a place to live, a car and I had my first good job. My daughter's dad and I weren't together anymore, but we were still good friends. I had a lot of respect for Charles. He took care of Lil Terry like he was his son and made sure we wanted nothing.

It was his idea that I go back to school and take up a trade. And I did. He was smart like that, always thinking ahead. On the flip side, anything I knew about the dope game I learned from him. I guess you could say he was that nigga on the Southside. A smooth talker and he had the Southside projects on lock with some of the biggest jugglers in the city.

We had been together for a few years, slowly trying to get out of the game. One of Charles's homeboys had recently gotten knocked off, and he wasn't sure if they were coming for him. I had become accustomed to having money and being able to do whatever I wanted. I resented the choices he made. I didn't want a 9-5 man. I wanted him to continue doing what he had been doing since we met. I liked the excitement, and I was attracted to the lifestyle. The cars, the money I wanted it all.

A lifestyle like this is what he had created with me. So, I wasn't trying to hear any of that shit he was talking about. The more he transitioned, the more I resented him for it. He wanted to get me to see the bigger picture, but I was determined to keep my lifestyle the way it was. Dysfunction was familiar or normal to me, and normal was dysfunctional as far as I was concerned. I wanted what I wanted, no if's, and's, or but's about it. We eventually broke up after I had too much to drink one night and didn't come home. Charles was no saint, but the mere thought of me being with someone else was something he couldn't handle, so he dipped. I think he lost faith in me, and in turn, I did the same. Our flame quickly fizzled out.

After Charles moved out, my house became the house where Jay would keep all of his money. He didn't trust anybody, except me. So, I made sure I didn't touch it without asking first. Over the years, I would occasionally run into our Lil' brother Micah even though he was adopted. After all, we were from the same family with our dads being first cousins, so it was customary to see him at family reunions and stuff.

However, because he did not grow up with Jay and I, I made sure my brother knew how much I loved and missed him. We quickly developed a tight bond. Micah looked up to Jay a lot, and after he finished high school, the three of us were able to reconnect, and from that moment on, we were inseparable. Our bond was unbreakable. We had each other back no matter what. I was my brother's keeper, and they were mine. They protected me at all costs.

Micah used to hustle in the Southside projects, so that is where you would find him most days, posted up at the corner store. I would occasionally ride through, but none of the people living there was familiar to me anymore. Everybody I knew had moved, and most of the people who lived there now were from across town. Low-income families, drug addicts, gamblers, and different clicks of niggas from different areas, was what populated this area now. The mixture was a recipe for disaster.

One day, Micah was shooting dice with this guy they called 'Black' whose baby Momma had just moved over there. He was one ugly nigga, and his complexion fit his name because he was black as charcoal.

They had been shooting dice for a few hours, and Micah was up by four hundred dollars. After about two more rolls, Micah decided he was through playing. He said, "Yo, I'm out dawg. I'm bouts to take it to the house." Black got mad because he didn't have a chance to win his money back. He started talking shit about Southside niggas being fuck niggas and how green all Southside niggas was. Micah would often laugh at everything, so he tried not to entertain him, but this nigga kept coming for my brother. Micah said, "I ain't gone be too many more fuck, niggas, my nigga." Micah said. Shiiiidd, you lost, and that's that! You can't win them all my G."

Black pulled out a pistol and pointed the gun at my brother's head and said to him, "Nigga, you gone be whatever the fuck I say you is." Then, he hits him in the head with the gun. "Nigga, what? Nigga empty yo' pockets and gimme my shit before I kill you". Black demanded. Micah said, "You got it dawg and handed over the money with blood gushing from his head. Thank God nothing happened to him that night. Black went missing in action for a few weeks because nobody saw him after that. Micah called me but quickly asked to speak to Jay. He told him what had happened and Jay was furious, I don't ever recall seeing him that angry until that day. "Who the fuck this nigga Bro.? Niggas got me fucked up bout my people." Jay yelled. "Bro, you done seen that nigga before, real black nigga, his baby momma live in the end apartment. "The one that was Mr. Green's old apartment?" I asked. I was inserting myself into the conversation.

"Yea, why?" Micah asked. "Cuz I think I just saw him, I just rode thru there, and I think I saw him sitting on the porch." At this point, Jay was boiling. He walked right out the door. On the way out, he said: "Meka, I'll be right back." My posture shifted. Stay put Bro, Jay pissed and he on the way over there." I said. "Yo', This Jay calling me on the other line Sis; I'll hit you back." Nervous, I said, "Okay, Ya'll, be careful, and call me later."

Later that night, Black's baby mamas house was shot up. Police didn't have any witnesses or suspects, and luckily, nobody died that night. I guess that was too close for Black's baby mama because she moved right after that. But things were not over between Jarvis and Black. Black now wanted revenge asking people about Jarvis and Micah's family and where they lived. Word returned to Jarvis that this nigga was asking questions, and Jarvis knew he had to find him before this nigga found us.

Jarvis always told me that all it takes is one weak link to pop a chain. Jarvis was willing to risk his life before he let anything happen to me or anyone else he loved.

Jarvis had a chick he used to fuck with at the apartments she was nobody serious; he used the house to trap. Not knowing that she meant nothing to Jay. Black saw her one day, walked up to her, and hit her like she was a nigga knocking her out cold. Females in the apartments were angered because everybody knew Jay had an old lady and a son. This girl ain't have shit to do with Black and Jay's beef. Jay knew he had to do something. He armed himself with two pistols and made his way to the apartment. He parked his car right under the 95 south highway located next to Douglas Anderson High school and started walking to the apartments. Jay had made up his mind that either he was gone kill Black that day or the nigga was gone kill him, but either way, the shit was gone end today.

Jay walked up the back street with pistols cocked and loaded.

As soon as he turned the corner by the stop sign to head to the lil store where all the guys would stand and catch the pops coming in the apartment, Black appeared out of nowhere and started shooting. Pop-pop, pop, pop, pop! Black let off 4-5 shots before Jay could pull his gun out. Jay quickly took cover, running, and ducking behind cars. Jay fired back, bang, bang, bang. It was like the wild, wild, west. Something you saw on TV. People scattered, trying to get out of the line of fire, and still, Jay and Black continued shooting at each other. Black managed to run in somebody's house. A chick named Nikki. Jay kept firing into the house, while Black was firing back. During the shootout, the girl was shot in the leg while holding her baby, trying to make it upstairs. Once she got to the top of stairs where her son was safe, she collapsed and rolled back down the stairs. There was blood everywhere. It trailed all down the stairs. He was seeing Nikki lying there unconscious, not knowing if she was dead or not. Jay stopped shooting and ran back towards the underpass where his car was. Black ran out the front door heading towards Philips highway.

You could hear police sirens getting closer, and before long, the apartment complex was surrounded by police with a helicopter circling above. My daddy, who lived a street over from the apartments, could hear the gunshots and police sirens from his house, but having no idea Jay was involved, he continued as usual. Thinking it was just another shooting in the hood.

Jay pulled up in the yard in a panic and rang the doorbell fast and repeatedly, 'ring, ring, ring, ring, ring, ring! When that wasn't giving him the response he wanted, he began frantically knocking, knock, knock, knock, knock, knock, knock!!! "Daddy, open the door!!"

"Boy, what the hell is going on?" My daddy shouted with concern. Out of breath and barely able to speak. He said, "This nigga Black just tried to kill me in the apartments, and I was shooting back at him, and I think I shot somebody. Oh, Lord." My daddy told him, "Stay here; let me go round here and see what's going on."

At that point, daddy was in a panic. He asked, "Miss Charlene, where the keys at? I gotta go, hurry up!" Miss Charlene pointed to the keys on the end table. He grabbed them and darted out the door. The police had yellow tape everywhere, and you couldn't go in or out of the apartments.

My daddy saw a lady that he went to school with crying hysterically and being consoled by a group of people. My daddy calmly walked over and said, "Gina, what happened? What's going on?"

"Them boys was shooting out here and done shot my baby in the leg. They say she gonna be okay, but lord they done scared me half to death. I'm waiting on my ride now to take me to the hospital."

"Come on; I'll take you," Daddy said. He told Gina that it was his son that was in the shootout and that he was sorry, and he didn't try to shoot her daughter. Daddy told her, "I know this is a lot to take in, but please understand my son was defending himself, and if he didn't fire back, he'd be dead right now." She understood and said, "Oh no, Rome. Why would your son shoot in my child's house? The nigga Black was trying to kill my son and ran in there, that's all I know right now."

When they arrived at the hospital, Nikki was in surgery. They were able to remove the bullet and said she would be fine but was still asleep from the anesthesia, and no one could see her except the immediate family.

Gina slept in the chair next to her daughter's bed until she awoke. "Baby, are you okay? She asked. Moaning from the anesthesia wearing off, she mumbles, "What happened? Why am I here?" Gina explained she was shot. "Nikki, do you know who shot you?" Gina asked.

"I saw Black running in my house shooting, and then bullets just started coming from everywhere." She struggled to speak. "I know he and Jarvis been beefing, so I think it was him outside shooting, but I didn't see him." Nikki was friends with the chick Black knocked out, so she didn't care much for Black. She was angry about Black hitting another female. When the detectives came in to speak with her, Nikki identified Black as the shooter. She could not identify the other individual. Police spoke to several people in the apartment complex, but all they got was the shooter was wearing all black. Nobody saw his face. Jay took care of Nikki once she came home from the hospital. He knew she could've snitched, but she stayed true to the g-code.

Black was apprehended running down Philips Highway. He had at least five charges stacked against him. One was carrying a firearm by a convicted felon, two, for shooting in an occupied dwelling, three, for attempted murder, four, for aggravated assault and five for fleeing the scene of a crime. He was off the streets and later sentenced to 35 years in prison. While he was in jail, he was stabbed to death by a Mexican during a fight. Karma's a bitch, ain't she!

Trap Bible 23:23 Lifestyle

Commandment: Thou Shall Be Down for Whatever

My cousin Rina and I had gotten close over the last few years. We lived in the same neighborhood, and our kids attended the same school. Our friendship was tight. If I wasn't at her house, she was at my home. Most people thought we looked alike. But I never saw the resemblance. Even as adults, people mistook us for twins.

Memories of me mistreating her as a child surfaced. There were times Taryn and I were mean, but in the end, I was glad I got to apologize for my part. She forgave me, and our friendship grew stronger. Rina had two boys the same age as my kids Terry and Asia. She and I reconnected after separating from our husbands. Yes, I was married.

Remember, when I shared the night's incident, I had too much to drink and didn't come home? Well, that's the night I met my soon to be husband, Chris. We dated for six years before we got married. He was well known and well respected in the streets. Some might say he was ruthless, but for me, he was a gentle giant. A giant soon to turn into a monster.

Chris loved to entertain loved having cookouts. We had the same friends. We traveled together, clubbed together, we did everything together. For the first time, I felt like my family was complete. I had everything I needed; two kids, a dog, a fenced-in yard, and a husband who loved me to death. No, we weren't perfect, but we both were happy, or that's what I thought.

One day, I was at home, braiding my daughters Asia's hair when the doorbell rang. I answered the door, and a small, framed, skinny white man with glasses and thinning hair was before me. "Yes, can I help you?" I asked. "Is this the home of Chris Miller?" He asked. "Yes, it is," I said. He said, "Thank you," and handed me a large envelope and left. Puzzled as to what it would be, I read the following: "The state of Florida and the petitioner vs. Chris Miller for the paternity of a newborn child." My happy home, as I once believed, was shattered. I was done; there was nothing he could tell me if this was his baby. Not only had he cheated, but he had cheated and fathered a child. Betrayed twice by men I loved. I think the worst kind of hurt is the kind that you don't see coming. You think everything is good, and everybody is happy, and then you get a harsh reality check that people aren't who they pretend to be.

Being abandoned as a child, walking away was easy for me. I protected my heart at all costs. No one would ever leave me again. Chris stirred up a fear in me, and before he had the chance to abandon me, I ended the relationship. I would soon learn the hard way. Everyone can't handle rejection. No matter how strong they appear.

Chris changed from a fun and loving husband to a complete monster. I was stalked, kidnapped, beaten, and raped by the man I married. I feared for my life, and he didn't fear anything, not my brothers, my ruthless daddy, not jail, and not death. He told me multiple times that if he couldn't have me, no one would. I didn't realize how serious he was until he broke into my house while I was asleep and set the bed on fire. He had completed six months in jail for violating the restraining order I filed against him. And to prove how angry he was, he broke into my home the very day he got out of jail. Yes, Ya'll, he was THAT crazy!

I had chosen a lifestyle that I was quickly growing to regret, and a man that now had me in fear of my life. My best friends Kira and Angie couldn't believe this was the same man who had us partying, popping bottles, and taking care of my kids and me. But he had everybody fooled. Kira and Chris were super cool. She even lived with us after moving back from Atlanta. Nobody could believe the person he had become. Kira,

Angie, and my cousin Rina were the only people I confided with about my situation.

I continued going to work with a smile on my face. No one knew my life was in danger. During this time, I realized Rina, and I had a lot more in common than I knew. We had similar situations that drew us closer. We would become inseparable.

Rina had become emancipated at the age of sixteen after being moved from house to house with different family members. But when life deals you an unlucky hand, you realize; it's still yours to play. And although life deals with each of us differently, how you play your hand matters in this game called life.

Rina's life appeared to be worse than mine. After her emancipation, she married a guy fifteen years older than her from California. His name was Rich. Rich was a big-time drug dealer. They had two kids, and he took care of his family. She had enough clothes and Coach handbags that would clothe an entire third world country if need be. Rina wasn't your regular 9-5 working girl like me. But that's not to say she didn't work Rina was in the game, and the game was in her.

Rina was a beast at cooking dope. She had gotten so good she didn't need a measuring cup. Rina knew the exact amount of baking soda to use to cut the coke. She would whip it so fast that the sound of the metal fork tapping against the glass cylinder is still, to this day, etched in my mind. Clink, clink, clink, clink! Rina would be so focused trying her best not to mess up Rich's package. Rina was so good in the kitchen that Rich named her the "cookie monster" He had taught her, and now she was better than him. Practice makes perfect, or Rich would be angry. And when Rich got angry, he often took it out on Rina. Busted lip, black eyes, you name it. She had gone through so much in her childhood, and now she was with an abusive, controlling spouse.

A Trap Girls Bible

Rina was smart. She had a plan, and she had a gift that most niggas in the hood needed. Rina wanted out of that relationship. And I owed it to her to help her. I remember how bad I mistreated her when we were growing up. I vowed to do better and make it right. She was my ride or die. I had her back, and she had mine. The only difference between Rina and me was that I worked and had my own money. Rich had been taking care of Rina since she was sixteen years old. He controlled all the money, and if she left, she would have nothing.

With Chris in jail again for violating his restraining order, I felt a sense of freedom, and I no longer had to look over my shoulder or wonder if he was going to sit outside the house for hours as he often did. Rina and I began orchestrating a plan to get her from under Rich's control. Each time he had a package that came in, Rina would keep about 28 grams and substitute it with baking soda so it would still weigh up the same. She would come over to my house, cook it up, and give it to my brother Micah to flip. Each ounce was worth about $2500-$3000 in the streets, depending on how big or small you cut the cookie. Micah would keep $800 to $1000 off each ounce and bring Rina and I back the rest. We were stacking our money and making plans to get her away from Rich.

Things were moving well until Jay found out who was fronting Micah the work. He wanted to be mad at me, and at first, he was furious. But Rina had now taught me how to cook. And as angry as he was, he knew that the two of us had skills. He was paying a nigga a few hundred dollars to cook his shit while Rina and I had become two of the best. His being upset didn't last long, and before you knew it, me, and Rina had linked up with and gained four of his homeboys. Now we was cooking all their shit!

Jay made sure to keep me and Rina's name clean. We had so much dope in my house that if anyone ever knew of it, I would have lost everything. My job, my kids, and my freedom. Both of my brothers had my back and vowed they would never let that happen. With Jay and the four clients we acquired, we no longer had to take anything from Rich. We had made enough money for Rina to move.

Now that Rina had her own money, she began to talk back and fight back. Rich had started seeing one of my cousins on my daddy side of the family. Rina and I were about to turn twenty-six years old. I guess she was too old for him now. Rich liked young pussy. My cousin, Ava, was only sixteen-years-old and still in high school when he started fucking her. That was the last straw for Rina. My little cousin was driving Rich's truck around town while he and Rina still lived together. Disrespect was a definite "no" in Rina's eyes.

One weekend Rich took a trip out of town and returned to a semi-empty house. Rina had taken everything she needed to furnish her two-bedroom apartment. But it didn't even matter, because Rina and Rich had so much furniture that the house was virtually fully furnished even after taking what she needed and wanted. Rich was furious when he returned. Unable to contact her and not knowing where she and the kids were, of course, my house was the first house he visited. Rich knew my brother Jay, and there would be consequences if he ever put his hands on me.

Bang, bang, bang! You could hear the burglar bar door. I looked through my peephole, and I could see that he was mad. He had a unit on his face, and his eyebrows were lowered into the shape of a V. With the burglar bar door still locked, I swung my door opened. "What Nigga?!" I shouted, "Where, Rina!?" He yelled. "I don't know, and if I did, I wouldn't tell you and slammed the door in his face. He shouted, "I know you know, where she at, so make sure you tell her I'm gone fuck her up when I find her!"

Two or three months had passed since Rina left Rich. During that time, he got a whore pregnant and had another baby. All while he and my sixteen-year-old cousin Ava lived together. Talk about a slap in the face! Rina's boys started to ask when they would see their dad again, but Rina was still fearful of seeing Rich. Although he had another baby and was living with another chick, Rina still didn't trust him. After a while, she finally decided to reach out to him after her oldest son *Lil* Rich had gotten into trouble for playing with matches in a vacant apartment, which almost set the whole building ablaze!

Rina and Rich started communicating over the phone about the boys. On one occasion, she felt comfortable enough to drop the boys off at Rich's shop. Surprisingly there were no problems or altercations. We assumed that he had gotten over Rina since he was no longer making threats. Rich continued living with my sixteen-year-old cousin, and he even took the boys to visit their newest sibling at his other chick's house. Rina thought they were in a good place, co-parenting. Keyword, THOUGHT!

Around 10 p.m. on a Sunday, Rina agreed to let Rich bring the boys home after visiting him. The boys had fallen asleep on the way home, so as soon as they got into the house, she escorted them to their rooms to not break their sleepiness. Rich had carried the youngest son Jeremy inside and put him in the bed as Rina accompanied Lil Rich, who was practically sleepwalking to bed. With both boys, asleep, Rina and Rich both walked out of the room, and Rina led him back to the front door.

As she reached for the doorknob, from out of nowhere, Rich grabbed a handful of her hair. He dragged her into the bedroom. "Let me go, Rich!" Begging him to let her go, Rich started to choke and punch her in the face. "So, you think you gonna just leave me, bitch?!" He continued his brutal attack. "Please, Rich, stop!" She cried out, and with all the commotion going on, *Lil* Rich woke up, and he came into Rina's room and saw his dad choking his mom. "Go back to bed. Rich shouted!" Knowing *Lil* Rich was watching, he stopped beating Rina and got off of her. He mumbled, "Bitch, you got lucky tonight and turned to walk out the door between clenched teeth.

In a panic, Rina reached into the drawer of the nightstand next to her bed and grabbed her pistol, a 38. The gun was recently registered. Rina fired two shots just as he was walking out of the door. Both shots hit him in the lower back. Rich fell to the floor, with half of his body inside her house and the other half outside. He rolled over on his back, looked at Rina in disbelief, and uttered, "You shot me?" As if he was unsure. Rina stood over him and was just about to put another bullet in his head, but again, Lil Rich entered the living room this time, saving his dad's life. "No, mama, don't hurt, daddy!" With a bloody face and one of her eyes swollen shut, Rina immediately called the police.

I was at home watching TV when the breaking news flashed across the bottom of my television screen. **"Man shot several times in the Mission Point**

Apartment Complex." It never crossed my mind the breaking news would have anything to do with Rina even though I knew she lived in the apartment complex. I knew she would have called me if she was in trouble.

The police had taken Rina and the boys down to the police station for questioning. I was asleep, and around 3 a.m., my phone rang. It was Rina, asking me to come to pick her and the boys up from the police station. Charges had not been filed.

I had so many questions. I was still unsure if I was dreaming or awake. Rina shouted, "Cuzzo, just come and get us, please. I'll tell you all about it in the car." Once I got to the station, she and the boys were sitting outside waiting on me. The police had released her gun back to her and called the shooting *Self-defense*. They informed us that Rich was alive. They would arrest him once he came out of surgery. The ride back to my house was quiet. Cuzzo stared out the window with tears rolling down her face, not making a sound.

We got back to my house and put the boys to sleep in *lil* Terry's room. It wasn't until we sat down in my living room to talk that I saw her face and how bad he had beaten her. I told her I wish she had killed him. We both cried and talked until we fell asleep. The next morning the detective came to my house to let us know he had made it out of surgery. And as soon as he was able to be transported, he would be taken into custody. He also informed us that Rich would be shitting from a bag that was attached to his bladder for the next couple of months.

Rina and I had been through so much, and it still wasn't over because soon, Chris would be out of jail, and I didn't know how he would act. And just as I was thinking about it, I received a notification that he would be released. But for now, Cuzzo and I were safe, click tight, and we had each other's back. Neither of us knew what the future held, but for sure, we were ready for **Whatever**!